CELTIC TALES OF MYT

By
A. E. I. FALCONAR

Illustrated by
CHARLOTTE J. HENRY

Published by
Non-Aristoteliean Publishing
Clifton, Slieau Lewaigue, Maughhold, Isle of Man

Distributed by:
England: Colin Smythe Ltd.

Printed by Ramsey Press 96, Isle of Man

TALES OF MYTH AND FANTASY

Preface

It was said of the Tuatha de Danann - The People of Dana, that they were a weird and mystic race that had never through the millenia relinquished their hold over the superstitions of the Celtic peasantry and still rule the spirit or fairylands, and reign in the caves and mountains, and the deep waters of the lakes.

The Tuathade Danann have another name and it is the Sidhe, and they are divided into two classes - the Shining and the Opalescent. The Opalescent are fewer than the Shining and hold the station of Princes of the Tuatha de Danann. The mystic poet AE described one of the Opalescent beings:

"There was a dazzle of light, and then I saw that this came from the heart of a tall figure with a body apparently shaped out of half transparent or opalescent air, and throughout the body ran a radiant, electrical fire, to which the heart seemed the centre. Around the head of this being and through its waving, luminous hair, which was blown about the body like living strands of gold, there appeared flaming winglike auras. From the being itself light seemed to stream outwards in every direction; and the effect left on me after the vision was one of extraordinary lightness, joyousness or ecstacy."

The Opalescent beings were exceedingly tall, whereas the Shining ones were only slightly taller than men, but beautiful and dazzling The vast mythical world of our ancient past that was marvellous and mystical is not yet gone from us; more and more people are conscious of the great loss to mankind, and are seeking to regain that world that people think was destroyed by civilization. But to the mystic it cannot be destroyed and in meditation beyond the senses we can all return there for it is innate in the World Soul which knows all things.

This book is dedicated to the memory of that long gone past and those regions beyond the World's visible frontiers.

CONTENTS

THE CHILDREN OF DARKLAND

The Tuatha de Danann were a people that ruled not only Ireland and all the Celtic lands but most of Europe as well. But like all races, the time of their decline came. And the King of the Tuatha de Danann desired a memorial to his race that would last for ever. Conaran the King knew that other races had made huge buildings and had buried their Kings in marble and stone but it was not material things but ideas of men that last for ever. So he brought together his sorcerers and wisemen and the witches and wizards at an assembly and he told them of his desire that the memory of their race should be preserved for ever.

The sorcerers thought for long and at last one of them named Cailidin, a man wiser than Merlin the wizard of later years, rose and spoke to the King in this manner.

"The decline of our race cannot be stopped for already the dust is covering our foundations and the moths are consuming the fabric of our lives, but it is not necessary to make a physical memorial. Though our decline cannot be halted, there is a way in which we can live for ever. We must hasten to our decline by entering the world of spirits before our time. We shall become a people of shadows but despite our frailness we shall be immortal and our deeds in life will be kept alive in our minds and in the minds of the races of the Earth"

The King did not like the thought of the Tuatha de Danann becoming a people of shadows yet he understood that it was better than decline and death; so he spoke to the huge assembly in these words.

"I have asked for a memorial and you have given me an answer that more than satisfies my question but it hurts me grievously to think that we who ruled much of the Earth and are still a great people must forsake the Earth and become a shadowy people. O you Wizards! Can you find no other way?'

But the Wizards though they spoke and considered for long together could see no other way. Then Cailidin, Father of Witches and Wizards rose and spoke again.

'0 King! What we have offered is not to make the Tuatha de Danann a frail and shadowy people but a very great one. We shall make you the Baghogh - The King of the Other World, and you will rule through time in Ildathagh. We shall be frail as the mist but our minds will be so magnified that no other people will be like us. We shall become a spiritual people living in the mind where there are lands to conquer far larger than the contemptible physical worlds of the universe.

The King Conaran pondered for some minutes and said 'Let it be as you have described it. The Tuatha de Danann will leave the world and go down

1

into the depths of the Earth, and we will become a shadowy people and we will rule the worlds of Ildathagh for ever.'

The descent did not occur at once but over the generations the Tuatha de Danann dwindled. They did not die but some of them were not seen again and some faded so they were shadows - creatures that could not be seen but cast shadows. And a day came when even these few shadows that remained melted into the mists of the mountains.

Mariners that came to Ellan Vannin from other lands spoke of it as an island of fallen houses and immense courts and palaces but empty of men.

Gradually other peoples began to replace the Tuatha de Danann, and the fields were once more sown and the houses were rebuilt.

But the Tuatha de Danann are not dead for they live for ever. Their abode is the mist of the mountains and they haunt the streams and caves. The Tuatha de Danann are as frail as the wisplike mist and like the mist they penetrate into the springs and find their way into the hearts of mountains. When the mist is thick and descends down the mountain sides, the Tuatha de Danann increase their domain and they come down to the dwellings of men.

A boy lived in the oldest and steepest part of Ellan Vannin - Island of Sheep and green valleys and mist and ancient secrets. The boy's name was Ian Cawdor and his forebears were military men and colonial administrators. His father was an army officer who spent most of his life on the frontiers of the world, so Ian was brought up by his grandfather, a man of the old school who practised a rigid rectitude and discipline. The old man was stern but kindly and no ignoble thought was ever allowed to be expressed in his presence.

While Ian's grandfather was still hale, they went together on long walks in the valleys and mountains, and it was under his grandfather's teaching that Ian gained a lifelong love of nature and his homeland. Furthermore Ian was brought up on the ancient stories of the heroes of old and the myths of the Island. So enthusiastic was his grandfather and so well did he speak that it was as if the Tarroo Uishtai still lived, and the little people still thronged the valleys; and it was from his grandfather that Ian first heard of the Tuatha de Danann.

The years passed and his grandfather became old and frail and no longer accompanied Ian on rambles; nonetheless Ian walked farther and farther into the mountains. His grandfather's house stood by the sea and a small stream flowed beside the garden. Ian followed the stream into the hills. At first was a coastal region of cliffs where he heard the sound of gulls and fulmars and the roar of the surf, and he soon reached a lush forested land which led to a steep gorge. For a mile he climbed beside a series of waterfalls and cascades that gave the impression of being a Chinese print so fragile and wisplike looked the birches suspended over the gorge. The gorge ended at a flat moor which at first

2

consisted of prickly broom that soon thinned and gave way to bracken and blue-berries. Here he could no longer hear the gulls and the sea and he had entered the moors of the curlew. Higher he reached bare rocks and the heather where mountain sheep and hares lived. The stream led him into a small sheltered dell full of caves and grottos. It was a place of whispering sounds and splashing water and the sinister croak of the ravens.

He had reached the place called in the ancient language. 'The Glen of Elves' Ian had been told by his grandfather that the old people of the Island spoke of it as sacred for it was haunted by supernatural beings. As Ian climbed still higher in the Glen, he sensed he was leaving the jurisdiction of men and was entering a world controlled by unknown forces. And now the mist covered him and he was reminded that this was the domain of Manannan, God of the ancient peoples. It was always silent here as if he had entered a sanctuary of religion. When he reached this place, Ian felt uneasy for he sensed that he was being watched and that he was beyond the help of men. Yet despite his uneasiness, it had an attraction for him that he could not understand; it was as if he was drawn to the Glen of Elves. He thought he saw movements out of the corner of his eye, and he remembered his grandfather saying that it is out of the corner of the eye that the little people can be seen; for they live just beyond human senses. When the head is turned towards them, they are gone for they move too quickly for the human eye. Now Ian thought he could hear a very small voice, and he looked about him but he could see nothing, and then the voice was repeated more clearly and Ian was sure of it and astonishment mingled with his fears.

At first Ian could see nothing and yet a vague spiral of mist was detached from the mountain mist that came and went in puffs and wisps. The voice came again from the direction of the spiral of mist. He could see vaguely the outline of a figure but it was hardly visible and it did not move and yet he was sure the voice came from it. And now the mountain mist covered him and the spiral, and the voice seemed far away and muffled. Ian waited and after a few minutes the mist cleared but he could see no spiral of mist and the voice was not repeated. He waited for some minutes perplexed and a little afraid and he left the Glen of Elves feeling cold and he was uncertain whether he had heard a voice or not.

He kept returning to The Glen of Elves and though he felt the sensation of being watched, he did not hear the voice for many days. A month passed and again he entered the valley and immediately he heard the voice and this time he was sure he saw a figure. It could not be seen directly but by looking to the side and focusing his eyes in a special way, he saw it not just as a spiral of mist but as a halo of colour. The figure was now much more distinct and the voice was clearer and he could recognise what it was saying. It was talking in

3

a friendly way and it said its name was Arawa. Ian felt reassured by its talk. They spoke for a long time but Ian could remember little of the conversation so strange was the experience of talking to a spiral of mist. When the mist cleared Arawa left or rather the spiral of mist that was Arawa evaporated into the air.

On clear days Ian nerver met Arawa but on misty days, Arawa was always waiting for Ian in the Glen of Elves. They had been meeting for over a year and a strong friendship had developed between them. And now Arawa asked Ian to come with him to meet his people under the mountain and to see their homes. A twinge of fear came to Ian for he remembered stories of human beings that were taken away never to be seen again. Ian was fifteen and his grandfather had taught him never to show cowardice, and the openness of his friend Arawa reassured him so he agreed to go.

They climbed higher still on the mountain and reached a small cave. The dark passage and the eerie whispering that came from its entrance frightened Ian but Arawa told him he had nothing to fear. So Ian followed his friend into the darkness and soon they heard other voices and they met a small group of Arawa's people.

They all walked down the passage which was dark at first but after having gone for a mile small lights set in the walls enabled them to see in the darkness. They went on for many hours and just as he was becoming very tired, they reached a stream beside which some small boats were lying. They divided themselves into three groups and launched   themselves into the stream.

They had now gone very far and Ian started to think he might never be able to return to the world above. He looked at his companions, and he thought that they seemed more distinct than they had been when he first saw them. The boats sped on and at last the stream fed into a large lake. And still the shadowy people did not rest or eat and Ian wondered if they did not eat and never grew tired.

His weariness had now increased so much, that he could no longer fear, and then the boats turned in the direction of a green light that was like a dawn. Soon the Sea of Emeralds as it was called became bright and before them was an island.

The boats grated on soft sand which was green and luminous. He picked up some of the sand and when he ran it through his fingers it glittered like particles of green fire and it astonished him that no heat was in the sand. The entire island was luminous and even the buildings and the paths shone with luminous particles.

Food was brought out and some of it was given to Ian. It was food that he had never tasted before though the fish and meat was not very different from what was eaten on the surface of the Earth. The rest of the food consisted of funguses and mushrooms and mosses and spores grown in the dark lands.

4

As soon as they had finished eating, they all prepared to sleep. They entered one of the huge houses and slept on marble floors on silk-like rugs. Ian was told that the Island of the Sea of Emeralds was not a natural island but had been built by the ancient Tuatha de Danann who needed a resting place mid way across the Sea. The foundations were of rock but the Island was studded with gems and the paths and houses were coated with emeralds. When the Tuatha de Danann built anything, it was made so that it would last for ever and this island was as beautiful as when it was first made.

They spent two periods of sleep on this island before they relaunched their boats and paddled onwards. The beauty of the island had distracted Ian from his fear, but when the island receded he became conscious that he was going still farther from his home. Now he sensed that his companions had grown still more or he had shrunk for they seemed no longer to be a shadowy people but had become as large and real as he was. So far had they travelled that Ian supposed they must have crossed under the sea and were under Ireland.

After many more hours of paddling, they reached the end of the Sea of Emeralds and they moored their boats on the beach and jumped onto the shore and entered a passageway that was brightly lit. Every few steps was a jewel in a crystal salver of liquid fire that was the jewel's source of light.

Now they began to climb and the heat of the low places in which they had descended was left behind and it was now less stifling At last they emerged into a vast hall at the end of which was a huge door of gold that was flung open at their approach. Guards in shining robes ornamented with jewels bowed to them and let them pass.

They went through more doors each more brilliant than the ones before; at each door were guards; and now they reached even larger doors shining with jewels too bright for the eyes to behold. Within the huge room were robed figures of extreme age on thrones. Contrasting with the splendour of the guards, the lords of Danaia were sombrely clothed for they thought of themselves as having passed beyond the pomp of men.

Ian and the small band of Danaians who he now realised were all young people like himself walked towards the leader of the Danaians and halted a few steps away from him.

The Great Lord of Danaia welcomed them home and speaking directly to Ian said, 'Do not fear us, we are men of an ancient people jealous of our honour and when we tell you that you will soon return to your home, you can be sure that it will be so. We bring you here for two purposes - one is so that we can inform the upper world of our history and myths and the other is so that after having returned to the upper world and when you are a man, you may wish to return to us and help us in our difficulties.'

He waited for some seconds and then slowly continued. 'Now you will stay with the young people who brought you here, and they will take you to the village of the children who will themselves tell you about the history of our people and the myths that we have preserved in our halls.' Ian was asked whether he had anything he wished to know before he went with the children. The only thing that still troubled Ian was the length of time he would have to stay in Danaia. In answer he was told that he would be kept no more than a few weeks.

Arawa who was a leader of the young people now took Ian away and he smiled at Ian reassuringly. These young people were not in awe of the Old men of the Council and Ian was to find that Arawa and his sister Findavir were direct descendents of the Lord of Danaia and they were Prince and Princess.

They left the sombre halls of the old men and walked lightly beside the River Rhiannon on either side of which were doorways like the entrances of caves in which the people lived, all except the Lords of Danaia in their halls of lead.

The river was not large but it was the lifeblood of Danaia for from it came all the water and the fish, and beside it lay the mushrooms fields and the mosses and the fungi that needed its moisture.

Arawa took Ian farther down the river until they reached the place where the children lived together. It was the practice in Danaia that when the children wished to leave their parents they could go to stay with all the other children who played incessantly. It was only a few hundred yards from the older Danaians and here were similar caves and it was to one of these that Ian was led.

The cave was not large but it was comfortable and on the floor were two mattresses of a silk-like fabric. At the back of the cave was a doorway that led to communal rooms for eating and recreation.

Almost at once it was time to eat and in Ian's honour a feast had been prepared. In the dining room, the children sat on mats on the floor. With Arawa and Ian was Findavir who throughout Ian's stay in Danaia was to accompany him. Ian was struck with astonishment for Findavir even at the age of about thirteen was beautiful. Compared to girls he had known in the Upper World she was not merely a Princess but a Goddess. There seemed about her a light or glow of blue fire for she was one of the shining people.

The place where they ate was large and here were many young people all dressed in robes of many colours of the same silken material he had seen in several uses. These young people possessed a serenity compared to young people in the Upper World. Their complexions were very fair like alabaster and their voices were soft and melodious.

At every important meal it was the custom in Danaia for a story teller to recite the old lays and tales of the Tuatha de Danann. The meal had not yet

6

ended when a poet of Danaia entered   the chamber and the children fell silent.

The poet addressed them in these words. 'Children, have you ever seen the wonder of the world behind a mirror? An even more wonderful world is behind the mirror of the sea, for the surface of the sea and every drop of water in the sea is a mirror. Only those who are partly mermen can enter and see in the half light in which those creatures of that mirror world are living. Amongst us are men and children who are not of the land at all but were once mermen. And now I shall tell you of their story.

The old mermen and mermaids are supposed to have died, don't believe a word of it. Like the casting of the skin of a serpent, they have cast off the shells of their bodies and have gone into the halls and buildings of a kingdom more splendid than any on the surface of the Earth.

In the very beginning was no separation of the two kingdoms and the people of the land and the sea moved freely in each other's territories, so that the land men could descend into the cities of the sea.

A God ruled the land and our own Manannan ruled the Sea, and there were many other Gods and above them all was the great Ruler of the Gods who lived amongst the clouds of the mountains.

Every year a festival of drinking and dancing was held when each God brought to the ruler of the Gods as a tribute some wonder from his domain. Every year the God of the Land brought a new animal and he invariably received the prize for the most marvellous creation. As the years passed, he became arrogant and treated the other Gods with disdain, so they conspired together to bring down the upstart.

First Manannan caused all the spinners of the spray, those mermaids that make the little wings of the water beads to stop their work. And soon a terrible drought was upon the land so that all creatures cried out and the God of the Land pleaded with the Ruler of the Gods to restrain Manannan for all the creatures were dying and the plants were sere and the Earth was opening into huge fissures. The Ruler of the Gods when he heard this, was angry with Manannan and told him to make the rain clouds return and pour their water on the Earth. So Manannan once more ploughed the sea and sowed the long furrows of the waves and threshed the sea fields. And soon the little water beads were flying into the sky and painting the canvases of the sky with clouds; and they made their little robes of many colours glint as rainbows.

Manannan was determined nonetheless to humble the God of the Land so he gathered together his craftsmen and built wondrous workshops in the crystal halls of the sea. And then at the yearly conferences of the Gods, his creatures won the prize for the God of the Land made ugly creatures like reptiles and insects, but Manannan made beautiful birds and graceful antelopes. He built the little martin like an arrow to fly between the continents and whose

*Blodeuwedd = Flower Face.   7

home is built in the shifting sand and thus it refutes the fears of men. And now the competition from the land craftsmen ended for the workshops of the sea and their craftsmen were far finer than those of the land. But rivalry still continued between the two master craftsmen of the Sea each of which strove to better the works of the other. Now one of them made a swift that was faster than all other flying creatures, and in reply the other made a tern that could fly for ever and would spend its life circling the Earth. And the first in reply was making a small machine that could fly between the stars. Every year that he was beaten by Manannan made the God of the Land more angry but he knew that he would never be able to find craftsmen on the land such as those of the sea. However, he thought that if he could capture some of the craftsmen of the Sea he might be able to make them work for him on the land. At that time no difference could be found between land men and mermen except in the left handedness of mermen and their passionate love of poetry and music.

The chief craftsman of the mermen used to come to the surface of the sea and he liked to walk on the sea shore, and here the God of the Land placed the most beautiful woman that ever lived. Her name was Blodeuwedd* and she had been made by the Gods, of flowers. When the craftsman came to the sea shore and saw Blodeuwedd, he was bewitched by her beauty and he vowed that he could never live without her, but she refused to go with him into the world beyond the crystal windows of the Sea. So, in this way, the God of the land enticed many of the Sea artisans away from Manannan together with their mermaids. And the God of the Sea closed the workshops and took the mermen far away into the deep sea. And furthermore he changed the mermen and mermaids so that they no longer had legs but in place of legs were given tails and fins like fishes so that they could not walk on the land.

He also cast a magic spell on them and they were made invisible so that they could be seen only in reflection in the sea; and they could be seen directly only by those who loved the sea and had formerly been mermen. You can tell a former merman for he weeps at beautiful things for they remind him of those cities beneath the sea.

The Sea craftsmen who had been taken to the land were now making beautiful things like the little humming birds and the butterflies and the flowers. But we shall never see again the work of the craftsmen of the Sea who have made their cities of the sea. We think of the coral islands, as being beautiful but they are made of the skeletons of insects whereas the grottos and houses of the mermen are made of wonderful things. They built cities of pearls and adamant lit by the light of fish that are the torches in the courts of the Mer Kings.

If you look on the shore you may still hear the sound of the workshops of the mermen. Even now they grind and crush the stones of the shore and draw back the green covers to show their precious works. If you lift a sea shell to your ear you will hear the sound of the songs of the mermen, for these shells are records, that lie broken on the sea shore.

And now Kerelya left the hall and Arawa and Findavir led Ian on a short walk before sleep. The story of the poet had made Ian think of the old fairy stories he had heard when he was very young. He felt a closeness to this happy people and he was no longer unsure of himself for he felt as one with Arawa and Findavir. It was as if he had known them all his life, indeed he had known Arawa for over a year. They told a few more of the ancient stories and then Arawa and Ian were so tired that they had to excuse themselves.

Ian lay awake for a long time despite his tiredness. He thought about this people who lived cheerfully in the total darkness and of their kindness and friendliness. Again and again he saw in his mind the beautiful face of Findavir. He heard the heavy breathing of his friend Arawa beside him and he at last fell asleep.

He woke and thought of the morning but here was no morning, yet the Danaians followed the rhythm of day and night. Arawa was not beside him so Ian rose and feeling exceedingly hungry dressed quickly and went to the eating room where he found Findavir who had delayed her meal to see him for they were to make a tour of the city together.

They met Arawa at the place where the children go to school. Arawa said, 'The classes take place at the edge of the river and the sand is the blackboard. The sand is not only used by the children in the classes but the day's news is written on it, These are rough drafts and it is an advantage that first thoughts and idle and trivial matters are scattered in the running sand and only things of lasting value are transferred to stone.' Arawa continued, 'The process of education is simple, we try to instill a desire for knowledge and enthusiasm and above all we teach creativity for this is the most important part of the happy and truly successful life. Finally we encourage resourcefulness and flexibility of mind so that the being will grow all its life. The children never fear to go to school for we teach in the way all creatures learn and that is by making a game of learning. For ultimately life is a great game. At first the children get little instruction except in the history of the race and in reading and writing and music and games and poetry. When they are about fourteen they are encouraged to take up philosophy which is a hobby of all Danaians. We try to find the strength of each child so that he will be able to grow in harmony with the true bent of his nature. At the end we try to lead children to a sense of the beautiful and the world of the transcendent.' The three of them spoke for a short time about the children who were playing happily near by and then left.

They reached a place where the Danaians made their robes and wove and dyed their cloth. Findavir said, 'The spinner of the thread is a small insect that is like a spider... It is a water spider and lives its life in the River Rhiannnon

9

where it sets its webs to trap the minute creatures of the water. The web has to sustain itself in the current and not be broken by quite large fish so it is amazingly strong. The strands cannot be seen by the human eye in the water or even easily in the air so they must be dyed before carding," Ian marvelled at this spider, this master fisherman who made the invisible nets out of his body, and how he swam all day at the edge of the river and like a human fisherman tended his nets and stayed at the edge in the shallows and cast his net for the drafts of microscopic fishes.

Findavir when she saw Ian admiring the spider and its nets, said, 'We have an old legend about the way the cloth from the spider was first spun and how it was woven. Long ago, a Princess of Danaia always played at the edge of the river with her friends the water sprites and the arachnids; and it was here, where the little ripples smile amongst the pads and lilies of the diatoms that she came one day in tears. And the arachnids made a little veil for her which was like a fine spray of water that hid her tears; but the Princess was still sad and though her tears could no longer be seen, she would not play with the water people.

The water sprites knew that she was sad because her lover had to go on a long journey in the Darkland, but they did not know how they could help her for they were only water folk. And the arachnids were also sad but they always knew what to do for they were always busy, so they suggested that they would weave a robe for her lover so fine that it would be like a mist about him and it would hide him from all his enemies so they would never find him.

But the little Princess though she was very grateful to the arachnids still wept because even if he was saved, he would never be able to find his way back to her. And the arachnids laughed for they had never heard of anyone being lost because they always attach themselves by their long climbing ropes to their homes before setting out, and even the smallest of the smallest arachnids were attached in this way so it did not matter how far they strayed, they would soon be found. The arachnids said they would make a robe for the young prince so that as he went on his journey he would let a thread out from the hem to guide him back to his princess.

When the princess heard the idea of the arachnids, her tears were stopped and her young man went on his long journey and returned safely and his robe was only slightly rent after the hundreds of miles he had gone so fine was the thread.

Arawa said, 'It is fortunate that these water spiders seem to be always dissatisfied with their work, for no sooner is one web finished than they start making another, and discard the first. If you look at the patterns of the robes we wear, through a magnifying glass, you will see the webs of the spiders. No human hand could weave such intricate work.

10

Now they passed on through the fungus gardens where the bulk of the Danaian food was grown. Nearby were flocks of sheep and goats, which were mainly brought up on fungi and water weed and dried fish meal.

The three of them now reached the centre of the City of Danaia and high above them were lamps like candelabra in which a small source of light was many times magnified by innumerable jewels. The light from the jewels did not seem very bright but it gave a sense of astonishing richness. Ian thought of the Arabs in whose gardens is always an abundance of water, for water is the most precious thing of the desert; and in the Darkland the Danaians had similarly made fountains of light for here it was light that was the most precious substance.

They looked at the place where people came to barter goods and buy and sell.

Ian said, 'Since they buy and sell do they have money for buying clothes and food or is it done by barter?'

'Money here is unimportant and the needs of the people are simple for we have hardly anything to spend money on. Nonetheless we do mint coins of tin and copper and silver and gold. Here the gold and what you call precious stones are the lowest valued coins for they are so common. All men and women have an allowance of money and this can be increased only by going on expeditions or for important service to the City. But this money is not so much that anyone becomes rich.

They had now completed the tour of the City and Findavir as she was to do during the whole of Ian's stay, started to tell him of the Danaian history.

'When the Danaians reached the lower World, they were at first very dispirited but soon under inspired leaders they found a new destiny and they began to prosper. On the physical side they tunneled and followed the underground rivers and they visited the most distant places of the Darkland. They were determined to make the most of their new world of darkness. Their numbers increased, and their land stretched almost endlessly both horizontally and vertically, and they threw out their outposts farther and farther. At last they built their city of Dana by the river of life that they called Rhiannon. They extended their passageways beyond the Rhiannon and the Lonely River as far as the Desert of Haria where no water has ever entered.

They went beyond the mines of the Ahergili the dead people whose origin and end is one of the terrible Secrets of the Darkland. They passed the Boiling Sea and they made pleasure gardens in Corahalyon and the Lake of Angharad. They went beyond the Hollow Mountain and the Lake of Fire.'

Ian listened while Findavir told him the stories of the Darkland and of the wisdom of the people of Dana.

The days passed swiftly and the time for his return to the Upper World

11

was approaching. A celebration was arranged for all the young people to wish Ian well and to speed him on his journey home. At the feast everyone was joyful except Ian who felt sad that he would have to leave these cheerful young people and especially Findavir who sat beside him. The Poet of Danaia rose to speak to the young people.

'When Ian crossed the Sea of Emeralds, he knew that some magical thing had happened to him. The world of the Tuatha de Danann is a sort of mirror world like the world of the Mermen. When he passed through the mirror in the Sea of Emeralds he saw the shadowy people grow as real as he was. Our land of the Tuatha de Danann is a world of the mind and it is still discerned in the Upper World; in fact many signs are there of the Tuatha de Danann. High on the mountains are the gardens of the Danaians that no one else cultivates. In the rocks is a mystic language written in runes of a material that will last for ever.

Conaran the King at the time of the descent of the Danaians into the Darkland pleaded with the Gods that the dancing girls at least be spared and allowed to remain on the surface of the Earth because of their innocence. And the request was granted for the dancing girls were always dressed in blue and red costumes; so the little girls were placed on the fuchsia branches and in the wind they dance for ever. But more than in anything else we have carved in the minds of the people ideas of the Tuatha de Danann. Runes have been written in the leaves of the mind as surely as they are written on parchment. Ian is a book written by the Tuatha de Danann and when he returns to the Upper World, though to himself his pages will be closed, the people there will read our story.

The days Ian was to spend in Dannia came to an end and he had to say farewell to Findavir for she was to stay behind while Arawa returned him to his home.

It was the plan of the Old Men in the Caverns of Lead that Ian would fall in love with Findavir and that his love would compel him to return to Danaia when he became a man. He was given a drug that erased the memory of his stay in Danaia from his mind, but one day when the effect of the drug wore off he would remember Findavir for she was one of the Shining Ones and she would command his loyalty and no other woman would ever gain his love as long as Findavir lived.

The group with Arawa leading wended its way through the long passages and they crossed the Sea of Emeralds and they paddled their boats up the river against the swift current. They reached the place where the boats had to be abandoned and the small group walked up the passageway towards Ellan Vannin.

When Ian emerged from the cave mouth he felt exceedingly weary and lay down to sleep in the bright sunshine.

When he woke his mind was hazy and he could not think where he was. The glare of the sun hurt his eyes that had been so long unaccustomed to strong light. He continued to rest and slowly his eyes adjusted and he was able to look about him. Still dazed he started to walk down the valley and he reached a place that he recognised and it was not far from his home. Later, he could tell his grandfather nothing of his adventures for his mind had no memory of it at all. It was as if he had had a strange dream.

THE BRIDE OF ELFLAND

A girl called Eileen lived in the time when Manannan was young and had not yet attained the Throne of Man. They first met as children and she remembered him always for she fell in love with him. Many years later they met again and by this time Eilleen had become a young woman and Manannan was struck by her beauty. But when she spoke, her accent was rough and her manners were uncultivated, and Manannan knew that she would be unhappy at the Court where she would suffer ridicule and be laughed at by the snobbish courtiers. So he treated her with disdain and she was dismissed from his presence.

Eilleen was a sensitive girl and her dreams had been broken by Manannan, and she felt she had nothing to live for any more. She left her home and without knowing where she was going, she followed a stream into the mountains. She walked for many hours and the river narrowed and she entered a gorge where the sides of the stream were steep and the course of the water became windy, and there were many waterfalls. She reached a place where the stream formed a horseshoe and dark trees with their branches leant over deep water. She was tired and she rested in this calm place. Soon her head fell back and the tinkling of the water sent her to sleep.

She woke up much later to the sound of music. She could not make out where the music came from but it was getting louder. At last she discovered the source of the music and it was a cleft in the rocks on the steep face of the cliff on the opposite side of the stream. It was not long before she saw emerging from the cleft one after the other, members of a band of pipers and flutists and drummers followed by other musicians with bagpipes and instruments she had never seen in all her life.

The musicians passed below her marching down the valley. Behind them came fairies in procession and these were followed by more and more important fairies. Then came a pause and large elves emerged who were the guards of Elfland, and immediately behind them came an old elf in brilliant robes with a crown on his head. Behind the King of Elfland came pixies and dwarves and elves in green.

Up to this time they had not noticed Eilleen who was watching with delight and a little fear.

The King was looking about him and suddenly he stopped as if he had sensed a stranger. Now he looked at her and she thought his eyes had gone straight through her so piercing was his gaze.

The King said to her, 'Who are you and what are you doing here? Don't you know this is fairy ground?'

14

He was angry but Eilleen was not afraid for she sensed that he was a kindly old King.

She told him that the man she loved had rejected her and she did not want to live any more. She said she was sorry if she had entered their land, she had not meant to disturb them and she asked forgiveness. The King of Eliland liked her gentle answer and he saw how beautiful she was and he felt sorry for her for she seemed to be a kind and courteous girl who loved fairies.

So he asked her to tell him about herself, and why she had left her home and come up to the mountains.

When she had told her story, he felt a desire to help her and he decided to take her with him as his daughter so that he would have her at his right hand for he had no children and even in fairyland it was sometimes lonely for the King.

So he said to her, 'Dry your eyes for I will look after you and I promise to marry you to Prince Manannan. But you must give me a promise in return. After you marry, for every six months you stay with him you will stay with me for six months also.'

The promise did not matter to Eilleen for she did not think the King of the Elves could persuade Manannan to marry her, for Manannan' s face had been determined and she knew that he would never change his mind. So she nodded her head and said she would gladly accept the bargain and go with him.

It was now autumn and the fairies' cavalcade was on its way from the mountains to their Kingdom Underwave. The roads of fairyland are the little streams which are peopled by Elfin guards who keep the roads of fairyland safe. To men they are roads with no signposts but the fairy people see plain signposts with clear directions that men never see.

The King gave the signal to move off and the fairy band struck up a marching tune and the cavalcade walked by the side of the stream that was called the River of the Elves, and they went down the signless roads, and they passed over many an elfin bridge and at the dawn they embarked on a fleet of fairy boats and they sailed away to an unimaginable land.

They reached the sea and beyond magic curtains through which no men see was the fairy world of Underwave. The magic gateways were opened like the drawing back of rainbow curtains and a shining world of crystal was revealed. The host mounted on steeds of dolphins and porpoises and sped along the highroads of the sea. Soon they reached the fairy grottos and the crystal halls beneath the covers of the Sea.

Eilleen lived in the Court of the King of Elfland and she was happy there for the folk of Elfland were kind to her and she was grateful to them for they were teaching her how she might win Manannan.

In the weeks that passed the fairy women taught Eilleen the arts of the courtesans of fairyland and soon her rough voice sounded like the silvern speech of elvish ladies. And now her posture became as straight as a Lord of Elfland for no mortal stands like an Elvish Lord. She learned to play fairy music that charms men's minds and makes men forget all cares. She learned fairy dancing so that her feet became light as thistledown. She was dressed in clothing made by the dwarves in the caverns of the Earth of material finer than silk.

Her hands could heal men's minds of sorrow. Her eyes gained the vision that lets them look into the souls of men and change their thoughts in sleep. She learned these and many other things for time in Elfland is not as time is on the Earth for every year on the Earth is as five in Elfland.

Eileen's foster father the King of the Elves became so proud of her that he boasted that she could be taken for a Queen of Elfland.

At last the winter ended and the time for the Elves to return to the mountains had come. At an assembly of the fairy folk, the King proclaimed the end of the Winter Court and the time for the journey to the Mountains. The trumpeters sounded the departure and the band of the fairies struck up a lively tune and marched off leading the cavalcade on its way. Swiftly they passed through passageways and reached the shore and the mouth of the River of the Elves where they embarked on the fairy boats. It was still night and few human beings heard the music for it is heard only by those who love fairies.

When they reached the horseshoe bend of the river, the King of the Elves spoke to Eilleen and told her that she was free to leave to win her Prince. He embraced her affectionately for she had become very dear to him, and the fairy folk all wished her well. Eilleen was greatly loved in Elfland for she had no airs and she was kind to all the folk of Elfland whether they were dwarves or fairies or elves or lowly pixies.

A group of Elves went with Eilleen to her home and then left her. Her Father and Mother were overjoyed to see her and they were amazed at the change in her and the wonderful clothes she wore.

A short time after she had come home, a grand ball was to be held at the Palace to which the young people of the Island were invited. But it was impossible for her to get a place near the Prince and she thought that she had been put in the high gallery deliberately so that she would have no chance of being seen by Manannan.

On the night of the ball all the people arrived at the Palace and Lords and Ladies descended from their fine carriages but Eileen's parents were poor and she had to come to the back of the Palace so that no one would see her. When she went up to the balcony her face fell for it was so high up that she could hardly recognise the faces of people on the floor beneath her.

The dancing started and she could see only a blur but she was able to pick out the Prince who danced with a succession of court ladies and seemed to be happy with each one of them.

Dance after dance ended and it was now nearing midnight and Eilleen was despairing of ever being seen, and she was becoming lonely and sad. It chanced that one of the young Lords who was a friend of Manannan went up to the balcony and saw the forlorn girl and he spoke to her and invited her down to dance with him.

Now with rising hope Eilleen descended to the floor and danced as no human being has ever danced. The touch of her hands and the look of her eyes made the young Lord's feet dance like an Elvish dancer. Suddenly all the other dancers stopped to watch. Some of the courtiers spoke among themselves and said no human beings danced like that; and others whispered that she must be the Princess of Elfland.

The Prince recognised the face of the girl that he had seen only six months before and he watched enraptured wondering where his friend had found her.

Later when he danced with her he became bewitched and he could remember nothing for he was bound in Elvish spells. When he looked into Eilleen's eyes his heart seemed to freeze and all those about him knew that he had lost his heart to the dancing girl of Elfland.

The days that followed were the happiest of Eilleen's life for she and the Prince were always together and it was not long before he asked her to marry him. But she was troubled and as the days passed and the time for the wedding drew near she felt more and more anxious.

She spoke to her Father about the promise she had made to the Elvish King. Her Father told her not to trouble herself about it for the King of Elfland would forget her promise. But she knew that the Elves forget nothing. She still wondered if she should tell the Prince before her marriage and again she was warned to say nothing; that she would be a fool if she told him.

Eilleen thought about it for a long time and she was a girl who loved the truth and she knew that her Father's advice was wrong. She feared also that Manannan did not really love her and he had been charmed by Elvish magic into thinking he loved her. She feared to tell him and yet she thought it better that he be told than for her to reproach herself all her life for having stolen a husband as a robber steals money.

Only a month remained till the marriage and the Prince and Eilleen were together and it was midsummer and she knew that half her time with Manannan had ended. She looked at him and the fear of losing him was very great but she steeled herself and said, 'You do not know some things about me, and if I tell them to you, you may no longer love me.'

He smiled at her and said that he would always love her

17

whatever she had done.

She said, 'You should know that when you rejected me nine months ago I was so heart broken that I went into the mountains and met the King of Elfland who befriended me. He said that if he was able to win you to me, I should have to spend six months of each year with him. But worse even than the bargain I fear that I have won you by Elvish magic and if it had not been for that we should not be marrying at all. You do not know that I am the foster daughter of the King of Elfland.'

Manannan smiled at her and said, 'I knew about your bargain with the King of Elfland, and though I do not like it, I am satisfied with it. If the bargain had been for you to stay in Elfland five years for every one with me, I should accept it. Furthermore you are wrong when you said I rejected you.I loved you from the first moment I met you. I seemed to reject you for I was told by a wise man that only by rejecting you would you be spurred to become a Queen worthy of the Kingdom. And the wise man was right for you were a country girl and you have returned a Princess of Elfland.'

After the wedding, Eilleen and Manannan were happy and the people of the Island were joyful. The days passed and the Elves did not come and Eilleen hoped that her Father was right and the Elves would forget.

One day they visited the farthermost bounds of Manannan's lands and Eilleen felt the near approach of winter and she sensed that she had not much longer with the Prince and she shivered and held his hand tightly for she dreaded leaving him.

She had hardly gone to sleep that night when in dreams she heard the fairy music and into her room came the sound of the fairy band. Her hand-maiden of Elfland came to her and said that it was time for her to leave. She kissed the Prince lightly on the forehead without waking him and stole away with the Elvish folk.

They went on the swift steeds of the Elves and reached the assembly place near the bend of the River. The King of Elfland took Eilleen in his arms and brushed the tears from her eyes and said, 'Do not cry! Your husband will not pine for you but be there to welcome you in a few months. And in that time we will train you further in our Elvish ways so that you will make him love you more than mortal man has ever loved before.'

Though she was still sad, the words of her Foster Father lightened her grief for he was a kindly old King and she loved him dearly.

When the Prince woke in the morning and found his wife had gone, he realised that the Elves had taken her away. He proclaimed days of mourning and sadness throughout the Island. No one was to smile and no flowers were to bloom, and no buds were to open on the trees or shrubs and no birds were to sing; and the Island became sere and even the sun hid his face and a dimness fell on the Island. Never had there been so long and so sad a time.

But eventually all things pass and the days started to lengthen and the Prince began to look forward to the return of his wife and he allowed people to smile once more but he did not let the flowers bloom until he should see Eilleen before his face.

One night some of the people who lived by the side of the River of the Elves heard the sound of the Elvish host and word was sent to the Prince. He straightway prepared the Palace for the return of Eilleen and he proclaimed rejoicing on the Island and there was to be dancing throughout the country and the flowers were to open again and the buds on the trees were to shoot and all things were commanded to be happy and the birds were to sing.

Manannan refused to sleep for he wished to welcome Eilleen himself when she came. He waited for many hours and at last he heard the fairy music that Eilleen had taught him. Through the palace gates swung the fairy band and Eilleen broke away and ran towards Manannan.

It was in April that Eilleen returned and spring came back to the Isle of Man and it has been so ever since for each year the Princess brings life to the flowers in the Spring and they fade when she leaves in the Autumn.

THE HOMA BIRDS

A poor fisherman and his wife lived by the sea, and they had two children called Diarmid and Cora. The family was very wretched for few fish were in the Sea and the father was hardly able to catch enough to feed the family. The mother became ill from lack of food for she often went hungry herself to feed the children, and she suffered from worry and loneliness. She had to be taken away to be made well and then it was far harder for the family; and the father had to leave the children to go fishing and sometimes he was away for days and the little children suffered from hunger and cold. One day the father went fishing and a great storm arose and the children waited and waited but their father did not come back; he would never come back. His boat had been overturned and he had been drowned. The two little children who were no more than babies were starving and they did not know what to do when a stranger came who had seen the wreck of the boat. He brought some food and told them that Diarmid would be taken away to a boy's home and Cora would be sent to a family who would look after her. He said he would return for them in the evening.

The two children did not like the man and wondered what would become of them. The frightened children went by the sea and tears were in Cora's eyes and they were sad for they had always been together and they feared that they would never see each other again. They looked at the sea through their tears and they saw only the ravening waves that told them how the Sea had killed their father. And they looked up at the sky wondering if in that vast place there could be someone to help two little children. Just as it was becoming dark two shadows passed over them and they were picked up from the sand and carried into the sky. Hour after hour they were carried higher and higher until they were above the clouds in a place where the sun always shines. All round them were birds with huge wings that let them fly for ever.

The children were brought to a nest of the Homa birds. It was spun of the substance of the air and the sunlight. It was like a cup in which the rays of the sun were collected. The inside of the nest was warm for it was lined with the silver down of the Homa birds which reflected the heat onto the birds in the nest.

In the middle of the huge nest was a pond in which were frogs and fish, and some vegetation was at the edge of the water.

The feathers of the Homa birds were transparent and their wings were like the wings of dragonflies so the soaring birds were nearly invisible in the sky.

The eyes of the Children were exceedingly sharp and all day long they

21

watched the soaring birds. The Homa birds looked after the children and treated them more gently and kindly than they did their own young ones. For when a Homa bird's egg is hatched and the fledgling comes out of the egg, it is thrown from the nest. But it is in so high a region that as it falls it grows feathers and becomes stronger and long before it reaches the ground it turns and flies up to its mother.

The Homa birds never touch the Earth and even when they are old, they fly away to their great city of the sky beyond the blue.

The children were happy for it was always playtime and the Homa birds were kind to them and no one told them to do what they did not want to do. In this place was no rain or darkness and the sky was always clear. Sometimes the Homa birds dragged their nests lower in the sky and they entered the tops of the clouds, here were small Homa birds like weaver birds that made the clouds and the mist. Millions of these small birds were between the long strands of air as if they worked at a loom. They made the beautiful chariot wheels of the snowflakes, and they designed the patterns of the ice crystals. Some of the birds gathered the silver light of the moonbeams and made it into the dew and let it fall on the trees and the shrubs and the spiders' webs. They made the hailstones as toys of the young Homa birds which were often spilt from the nests on to the Earth.

From time to time they passed nests from where other Homa birds came to visit and to tell wonderful stories of the sky.

One day they saw a marvellous sunset and the Homa birds told the children that the nests sometimes became old and frayed and had to be burned. The fire on the horizon was a pyre of the Homa birds' nests.

The food in the pond was replenished by water spouts and whirlwinds that brought up all manner of creatures such as frogs and fish and insects from the Earth. The Homa birds flocked round water spouts like gulls in the wake of a ship at sea.

One day the children were taken far away and they reached a place of the sky where the King of the Homa birds lived. He had eyes that could see beyond those of eagles and falcons so that invisible himself, he had seen the suffering of the two children when they lost their father and he had ordered that they be brought into the sky. The King of the Homa birds was larger than all other birds and he was wiser than all creatures of the Earth, and he loved little children.

He looked at them with kindness from his throne of spun air that shone golden in the sunlight.

He said, 'There are children of the land and children of the sea, and now you know there are children of the air. I will tell you the story of how we came into the high places. Long ago when the Gods were young and they still

22

lived on the Earth, all creatures were not as they are now. The Homa bird dwelt on the Earth but even then he loved to soar in the sky as the eagles soar now.

One day the King of the Gods ordered that all creatures of the Earth should come to a great assembly where he wished to address them. When all the creatures had arrived and a roll call was taken, it was found that the Homa bird was missing so a small messenger bird was sent to fetch him. It took so long to find the Homa bird that the Gods became impatient and the meeting started without him. The King of the Gods spoke for a long time and just as he was finishing, the Homa bird arrived. The Gods were angry and said they would punish the Homa bird; and since he loved the sky so much, henceforth he would live only in the highest regions and would never again touch the Earth.

The work of the sky was given to the Homa birds. When the God, of the Sea Manannan needed help against his enemies who wished to attack the Isle of Man, it was the Homa birds that spun the fine mist and let it fall over the mountains and the valleys like a veil over a woman's face, so that no one could find the island in the huge ocean.

Long before the Gods had banished the Homa birds from the Earth, Winged Goddesses flew over battlefields and brought the souls of heroes to the Heavens of the brave. The Homa birds were given this work to do, and still they watch over the brave; and they care for little children who have no one to look after them.

The children were tired from listening to the King of the Homa birds, and despite their love for him, they could not keep their eyes open and they fell asleep.

The King of the Homa birds smiled with compassion for he was very wise and he instructed the messengers to take the children to their nest.

The children became more and more happy and they forgot the misery of their life on the Earth, and they thought only of the love that the Homa birds gave them. As the years passed they learned many things from the Homa birds. They also became much stronger and
their eyes became keener so that they could see a different sort of Homa bird far up in the sky, which seemed to be pinned to the heavens.

The bodies of these Homa birds were no larger than those of humming birds yet their wings were the size of condors' wings. One of these birds fell with a broken wing. It was like a huge canopy that had fallen on their nest. The children helped the big Homa birds fold its wings and mend its broken bones. When it was well, they launched it like a kite into the sky. Slowly it soared into the heavens and they thought of it as a living silver kite and it was as if it was absorbed into the air for they saw it no more.

Once again they were taken to the King of the Homa birds who said to them, 'You have now learned to see the Homa birds that fly above your heads. But higher still are Homa birds that can never be seen. They are the swiftest of all birds called Martlets that fly between the stars. They think of our Earth as only a way station on the roads lit by the beacons of the Stars.

The speed of the Martlets is faster than thought yet out great city of the Sky takes uncountable days' journeying for the Martlets to reach it. They go to places far more wonderful than the Earth. Every night in sleep, you are taken by the Martlets to a land of dreams.

'Yes, children, we go to many lands of dreams. One of them is a land that is the most wonderful of all, where eyerything we think and are is reborn and lives again.'

The King of the Homa birds told them many things but they became tired listening to the wisdom of the Homa birds and they fell asleep. Once more they were returned to the nest by the messengers.

The years passed swiftly and the children were happy but they were so well fed and cared for that they grew too large and heavy for the nest. Their feet kept going through the fragile sides of the nest and the danger was that Diarmid especially would fall right through and it would have been difficult for the Homa birds to bring him back into the nest so heavy had he become.

Now so much fear was felt for the children that they were brought to the King of the Homa birds. He felt sorrow for he did not want the children to leave him but he knew that he could do nothing else and they were now strong enough to look after themselves so he spoke to them for the last time.

'I told you long ago of a land of dreams to which we will take you when you are old. But now on the Earth if you are tired and fearful remember us who are your friends high in the sky. Be brave and good and we shall watch over you. I have to say farewell but never doubt that we will meet again where the dreams ripen in the harvest fields among the stars.'

Now the messengers of the Homa birds were summoned and the children were supported by the feathers of the Homa birds and they floated down through the night with the messengers guiding them.

Down and down they floated through the dark and at last as the dawn broke they reached the Earth at the same place from which they had been taken long ago.

As they walked towards the little cottage, they saw smoke coming from the chimney and a woman came running towards them and it was their mother who was well and strong. They were happy together and they never again felt the fear of being parted. Cora and Diarmid grew up and they were always happy and even when they had reason for sadness they would look up to the sky and they knew that high above their heads was their friend the King of the Homa birds who could see them and was looking after them. And they knew that one day they would be carried away with him to the Great City of the Sky.

IDERL THE MERMAID

Long ago in the Isle of Man lived a King whose name was Tura and he was just and ruled kindly and the people prospered and were happy. In due time, Tura's Queen gave birth to a son who was named Aran and rejoicing filled the Island because an heir had been born to continue the line.

By the time the young Prince had reached manhood he had proved himself brave and resourceful and he was respected and loved by all the people of the Island. He was also handsome and many tongues were wagging amongst the women of the Island and not one of the noble ladies of the Court did not hope that she would be the one chosen to marry the Prince.

However the Prince saw a vision and it showed that he would marry a woman who would come from the Sea. The soothsayers tried to interpret his dream and they said he was destined to marry no ordinary woman but a lady of a magic people.

He spent his days in manly sports and in the arts of warfare and hunting; and his Father the King made him work and learn the skills of husbandry and farming. The Prince was also sent out to Sea with the war fleet and the fishing fleet. The fishermen were glad to be accompanied by the Prince for he understood the minds and ways of fish and he brought them luck in the form of bountiful catches of fish

One day he was leading the fishing fleet and it was as if he was told where he must go to drop the nets. He immediately ordered the fishing to cease and the nets to be raised and to the wondering fishermen he said that he saw a vast shoal of fish in the West. They sailed away from the Island and rounded Ireland and they went farther than they had ever sailed before and the fishermen marvelled at their Prince and they feared for their lives. At last he ordered the nets to be dropped and the fishermen knew at once that a huge shoal of fish would be caught.

The laughing fishermen struggled with the nets and they were hardly able to bring them to the surface of the sea.

The bursting nets were at last in the boats and the tired fishermen and the Prince looked at the mountains of fish.

They were about to leave for home when the Prince saw a light that appeared in the depths of the sea. He told the fishermen to bring the boat over the light and to lower a net.

As the net was raised, the light grew brighter and they could see it distinctly not far below the keel of the boat. They could see vaguely the outline of a human being that seemed to be luminous and shone with a blue light. When the net was raised above the surface of the water, the Prince was astonished to see the figure of a woman who held a small lamp in her hand, and as soon as she saw the fishermen. she dropped the lamp and the brilliance of it faded and it slowly extinguished as it sank. The dimming of the lamp ended the magic and wonder of the woman from the sea and she became changed and had the form of a young woman. Her clothes were oily rags that were frayed and her hair was long and black and streaky, and her skin was pale like coral. The fishermen quickly brought her into the boat and they were filled with amazement for though they believed in mermaids, they had never dreamed of one with feet and legs like a human being, furthermore she was more beautiful than any woman they had ever seen.

The Prince remembered the prophecy and he recalled the beautiful face of the vision and it was the same as the mermaid's.

They sailed the long journey back to the Island with their boats low in the water, and the Prince brought the mermaid to the Court to show her to his Father the King. The ladies of the Court saw how beautiful the mermaid was and they became jealous and angry, and pretended to be contemptuous, and they laughed at the little mermaid because of her tattered clothes and her hair that was like seaweed. The Queen hardly stopped to look at her but left saying the mermaid should be thrown back into the sea.

The King who was kind to all creatures instructed the Chancellor to send teachers to teach her to speak, and clothes to dress her and hairdressers to attend to her hair.

On the next day when the mermaid was brought to the Court she was even more beautiful and the Prince fell in love with her and asked the King to give his permission to marry her. His mother, the Queen, was angry and told the Prince that he must only marry one of the noble ladies of the Court not a waif cast ashore by the Sea. The Queen sniffed and said, 'She is no more than flotsam of the snorting sea'.

The King also sought to dissuade his son saying, 'It is not for a son of a King to marry anyone he finds for he must consider his subjects and what is good for the Kingdom. I will not allow you to marry a mermaid of whom we know nothing.'

The Prince was determined and spoke vehemently to the King, 'It is known to everyone that the vision foretold that I must seek my bride from the Sea, and how can I avoid my destiny whether it is good or evil? Surely this coming of the mermaid is what was prophesied and I will marry her even at the cost of the Kingdom.'

The women of the Court were even more jealous when they learned that the Prince had rejected all of them and wished to marry this mermaid, a creature not even of the land but a weird being of the deep. Rumours were spread that she was magical and would vanish as suddenly as she had come.

27

Some said she was a temptress of the devil and would lead the Prince to Hell.

Iderl, for that was the name of the mermaid, soon learned to speak the language of the Island and she and the Prince often talked together and he was never more happy than when he was with her and she with him. The stories of the women of the Court came to the ears of Aran and he heard many evil things about her, but in talking to Iderl he found that while many spoke ill of her, she spoke only well of others. He found that she had a mind that could not think of evil. He knew the rumours were wicked lies and that she was innocent of wrong doing.

The Queen never rested from trying to stop the marriage of Iderl and Aran, but all she did made him more determined than ever.

At last the Queen went to the King and spoke to him in these words, 'It was customary for women to give dowries to the parents of the bridegroom. Let us set aside a day for the exchange of gifts. If the family of the bride do not give suitable gifts, it will show that she comes from a family of paupers and it would be unfitting for the son of a King to marry such a woman. I want you to give me your word that your son the Prince will not be allowed to marry Iderl if the dowrie is insufficient.'

The King thought that dowries were a wicked custom but in spite of being a strong leader of his country, he was like wax in the hands of his thrawn and domineering wife, and he reluctantly agreed to her proposal.

The day for the exchange of gifts came and the presents of the Prince's family started to arrive with the first sign of the dawn and they continued to come throughout the day. Horses and cattle and sheep and jewels and articles of silver and gold and wonders came from all the countries of the World. But no presents came from the family of the mermaid.

All day the Prince waited becoming more and more sorrowful, so forlorn and sad did Iderl look. Her large eyes were full of tears as they followed him fearfully for she knew she would lose him. The King saw the Prince and Iderl, and he felt compassion for them and bitterly regretted his weakness in giving in to the Queen.

The sun was setting and the Prince had given up hope when an old man was seen to come from the sea shore bearing a wicker basket of the sort that poor fishermen use, and he came to the Palace gate. The guards turned away so dishevilled an old man, but Iderl had seen him come and felt sorry for him and ran to the gate to see what he wanted.

The old man spoke a few words to her and gave her the basket and left. She took it to the chamber where the gifts were to be opened, and where the Lords and Ladies of the Court had assembled.

King Tura commanded that the gifts should be shown. Iderl opened the basket and brought out some shells and placed them round her. She looked like a little girl on the sea shore playing with some broken shells. The women of the Court in their cruelty and hatred scorned her and laughed at her and her despicable gifts. On the face of the Queen was a look of malice and evil triumph and she scowled at Iderl. Then she beckoned the ladies imperiously and they followed her out of the chamber.

When all the Lords and Ladies had left and the Prince and Iderl were alone, the Prince's heart filled with pity for her and he went to her and kissed her and he said, 'Even though I may never become King, it does not matter, for I shall marry you and we will be together always.'

She said to him, 'How kind and generous you are to love me despite the ignominy and scorn you suffer for me. One day I will repay your kindness with a gift of the Mermen that unlike these human gifts will never perish. But now I have only these poor things to show my love for you.'

He supposed the gift of the Mermen she spoke of was only a tale and he slowly and sadly took from her hand the shell she offered him and he opened it without hope. Inside the shell was a pearl larger than any he had ever seen. He took it to the light to see its lustre and he knew that it was the finest pearl that had ever been seen by men. He looked at Iderl and marvelled for it was worth more than all the gifts that filled the palace.

She said, 'In the Kingdom of the Mermen such things are of no value, they are given value only by the greed of men. These pearls were the humble gift of the oysters to the King of the Mermen, and even if men were to scour the seas for ever, they would not find such pearls as these.'

And now no obstacle seemed to be in the way of the Prince and Iderl marrying but the Queen was still raging. She said to the King,
'Although the pearls are worth a king's ransom here on the surface of the Earth, they are said to be worth nothing in the regions of the Mermen. Will you let them buy your son for a few baubles? Let us make sure our future daughter-in-law is worthy of him. Enquire of her what her Father is and his Father before him was and how many generations they went back like you with your five generations of Kings."

The King became angry for he found his wife's talk distasteful but something he did not understand made him agree to her scheme, and he said to her, 'Again I let you have your way, but it will be the last time and no other test will be made of the mermaid. I find no fault in her for she has always behaved with kindness and courtesy and she has looked like a Princess of a great Kingdom. Furthermore I fear it will rebound upon your head and we shall be made to appear petty and mean.'

So the King asked Iderl to tell him how many forebears she had and what was her lineage and state. Even as he spoke he felt remorse and he wished that he had not given in to the Queen.

Iderl said, 'Since I was a child in the Court of the King of Merland, no one ever talked of such things. But if it is necessary, then a messenger can bring the answer.'

The King felt sad and embarrassed but conscious of his promise to the Queen, he ordered the message to be sent.

The day of the messenger's return came and again the Court assembled. The Royal parentage of the Prince was proclaimed showing that when he reached the throne, he would be the sixth of his family to ascend the throne of Man.

Instead of an old man coming from the sea shore, a delegation of the Noble Lords of Merland arrived at the Court in magnificent clothing shining with jewels such as had never before been seen in the Court. All who saw the Merlords were amazed and startled by their appearance and the power of their presence and a silence of awe fell upon the Earthlings of the Court.

The leader of the Merlords stepped forward and spoke to the King announcing the purpose of their visit which was to present a scroll on which was written the lineage of Iderl Princess of Merland. The King took the scroll and instructed the Chancellor to read its contents to the Assembly.

'Greetings from Edera King of Merland to Tura King of Man. I affirm that the Princess Iderl of Merland is the true daughter and heir of Edera whose lands are of the Sea and the Southern Ocean. The lineage of the Kings of the Sea stretch back unbroken into the mists of time before human history for Iderl is the hundredth generation of the line of the Kings of the Sea.

I further proclaim that while you subjected Iderl to material tests, I have tested your son Aran the Prince, not with material tests but spiritual ones. Thus it was that I sent Iderl as a poor mermaid and few of the proud Princes of the World would have taken her in that form and made her his Queen. But Aran your son has proved that he is a noble and generous and brave soul, and I give my daughter to him gladly.'

Then the leader of the Merlords spoke again, 'It is the command of the King of Merland that a jewel be presented to Iderl, which shall be called the Jewel of Iderl. For Iderl in the language of the Mermen means jewel of the sea. The wonder of this jewel is that it gives light but only for a Princess of the Mermen. This is the last proof that you sought of the state and heritage of Iderl our beloved Princess of Merland.'

When Iderl took the jewel in her hand, it became a lamp and when she held it above her head, the hall became bright as day. But when the Queen took the jewel it went dark and dull and none of the noble ladies of the Court could light the Jewel of Iderl.

The ladies of the Court were overwhelmed by what they had seen and fell silent and their opposition to Iderl ended but the Queen felt humiliated and her mean soul was still wrathful and bitter.

The King could not contain his joy and he announced the day of the marriage and he was full of gladness for his son and for Iderl. The Nobles of Merland were royally entertained and they stayed to witness the marriage.

For many years Aran and Iderl spent happy and carefree days and their joy was still further increased for two sons were born to Iderl. But now the King and Queen had grown old and when they died, the Prince became King of the Island and Iderl was his Queen.

Aran was good and just and ruled with wisdom and the Island prospered and the people were content. Always at his side was Iderl who offered gentle and kindly counsel and she was greatly loved for it was said of her that she was a Queen who loved all people the great and the small without distinction, and she was kind to all creatures and hated only pride and cruelty and conceit.

Though the King Aran grew older, it was seen that Iderl did not change and she was the same as when he first met her. All round her men and women were growing old but she still possessed the fresh cheeks of a young girl and no wrinkles were on her body. Time could not touch Iderl. The years passed swiftly and the King became old and troubles came to the Island. The fishing boats did not catch fish for Aran could not go out to Sea any more so frail had he become, and the harvests failed and starvation came to the Island. King Aran grew thin with worry and he suffered with his people and Iderl felt sorrow for him.

And now murmurings started against the King for the people forgot the years of prosperity and remembered only the years of want and misery. Many spoke openly against the King and rebellion broke out in the South of the Island and the ringleaders captured the King's elder son and proclaimed that it was time to depose Aran and crown his son in his stead.

The rebels were victorious and defeated the King's forces and King Aran was forced to flee the Island and he took refuge on the Calf of Man with Iderl and their younger son.

King Aran looked even older and sadder for all his possessions were lost and his dreams had been shattered. Above all it mortified him to see his wife in a poor shepherd's cottage eating rough bread and water and wearing coarse clothing. He looked at his younger son and was still sadder for the rich promise of his son would end in exile and penury. The Calf of Man was cold and windy and it seemed to Aran that the Sun had set for ever for him and he wished only for death.

Iderl never changed for the riches and good fortune of men were hateful to her. She always knew herself as having come from a far more wonderful Kingdom. Nothing in the world of men could trouble the serene spirit of Iderl the Mermaid.

Her only wish was to relieve the suffering of her husband and to correct the misfortune that had befallen her son so she said to the King, 'Long ago I promised you a gift hidden from all men, an eternal gift. When I first lived in the Court of the King of Merland it was prophesied of me that I would go up to the world of men and marry one of the Princes of the Earth. So it was that I swam to the surface of the Sea, and it was ordained that you would be guided there and I would be caught in your net. I am not of the Land but of the Sea and I have only been loaned to the Land for a period of time and that time has now ended.

'It was said of me that not only would I return to the Sea but my husband and my younger son also.'

So the three of them came to a grotto of the Sea and Iderl showed them how to part the curtains of the Sea and enter the crystal passages that lead to the lands of the Mermen.

Many days they walked and at first the King was exceedingly weary and he leant on Iderl and his son but as they journeyed he grew stronger and he cast aside his staff. The dimness went from his eyes and a spring came into his step and long before they reached the coral gates at the outpost of the Lands of the Mermen he was no longer an old man but he had become as young as he was when he first met Iderl.

They entered the Court of the Merlords that was built by the coral insects and was more wonderful than the coral atolls of the Sea. King Aran beheld a court so magnificent that he was overcome with awe and wonder. Through the crystal windows of the Court were many shining fish which were the lamps that lit the halls of the Merkings.

The King of Merland was overjoyed to see his daughter again and the nobles in whom was no jealousy or avarice stood and were filled with delight at the coming of their beloved Princess and her consort. King Aran and his son were welcomed into the Court of the Merlords and they soon forgot the misery and misfortune of their troubled Kingdom, and they were happy and it was as if sorrow and despair could not live in the land of the Mermen.

Iderl and Aran were not left to enjoy the quiet joys of the land of the Mermen for long. Not many months had passed when King Edera called them to an audience of all the Merlords, and he addressed Iderl in these words, 'Though I am young in appearance, yet I am exceedingly old and I am glad that you have returned for I have become weary of my duties and I desire to shed them from my shoulders. So much did you do and so much learn in the world of men that without delay I wish to pass those burdens on to you.'

So Edera stepped down from the throne of Merland and Iderl was crowned in his stead and Aran was her consort. They ruled the land of the

Mermen for many years and at last they also tired of the honours and duties and passed on the Kingdom to their son.

It could be said of Iderl and Aran that never again did unhappiness come near them.

THE DREAM BOY

Once an orphan boy named Duncan lived in a town in the Isle of Man. After his parents died, he was sent to stay with foster parents who did not like him and treated him cruelly, and they always tried to show him that he was inferior and more stupid than his foster brothers and sisters.

All the people in the town knew that he was an orphan and his foster parents spread bad reports of him so that people scorned him and there were no friends for Duncan.

When he became older he was sent to school, and the boys were even crueller than the grown ups, and they thought of him as different and he was bullied ceaselessly.

Duncan tried to stay away from the children as much as he could and he never played with them. He learned nothing at the school for his thoughts wandered from work to the wild play grounds of his mind. The Schoolmasters beat him harshly for they supposed he was lazy and wilful.

But life was not all sadness, for Duncan learned to think and dream, and in his dreams he went away to a wonderful land. As time went on he strayed further from the people of the town and his dreams became more real and he went on longer journeys into Dreamland. He spoke with the people of Dreamland and they were not like the people of the town for they were kind to Duncan, and he was always happy when he went to Dreamland.

One day after school, the boys were bullying him and one of them said, 'What do you do all the time thinking and dreaming?'

And he said, 'I go to Dreamland and I walk in the beautiful cities there and see the wonderful gardens where music fills the air. It is a place far finer than this town or this Island.'

The boys said he was mad, 'If you really go to Dreamland then bring us something back from there.'

They all laughed at him.

But the Dream Boy said, 'What would you like me to bring back?'

The boys thought for a moment and then one of them said, 'Bring back something that the dream people have made.'

The boys went away laughing scornfully and ridiculing the Dream Boy. That night he was in the streets of Dreamland and he asked one of the women he met if she would give him her brooch to show to the boys of his school. The woman of Dreamland was not sure if she should give him her brooch but she felt sorry for him and let him have it..

When he woke in the morning a small brooch was gripped tightly in his hand. He showed it to the boys at school and they were envious for they

34

could see its marvellous workmanship. They took it from him and ran away with it. He told them it was not his and they had no right to take it from him. But the boys sneered in his face and laughed at him calling him a fool.

Some weeks passed and the boys tired of the brooch and one of them left it at his home; the boy's father saw it and he was amazed by it for he knew it was not made by human hands and he saw with astonishment strange writing on it.

The brooch was taken to the elders of the town who made enquiries to find out the owner of it.

The Dream Boy was brought before the elders and he told them how he went on a dream journey and brought back the brooch to show to the boys at school. The elders did not know what to believe but one of them sneeringly told the dream boy to go back to Dreamland and bring him a jewel from there.

The little boy went home and that night he found the treasury of Dreamland and chose one of the jewels.

When he woke in the morning a small jewel was in his hand. It was brighter than a diamond and it shone in the light like an ember from a fire.

The elders were amazed and a jeweller said it was the most dazzling ruby he had ever seen. Some of the elders were troubled and they looked at the Dream Boy with suspicion as if he was evil. And some of them were greedy and they desired to possess some of the jewels for themselves. The cruel foster parents took the jewel away from the Dream Boy and they told him that he must bring them back a jewel every night.

Each morning Duncan woke up with a jewel of a different colour in his hand and soon the foster parents became rich. Instead of being grateful to the Dream Boy, they became envious and even more greedy and they told him that he must bring back larger jewels not the small ones he had been bringing.

That night the Dream Boy did what his foster parents told him but despite trying hard, he had not the strength to bring back a large jewel. Each time he lifted one up it seemed to be snatched from his hand and fell to the ground. Time after time he picked up a large jewel and each time it was taken from him. He became tired and it grew dark and he could no longer see the jewels and fear came to him for he wondered if he had done wrong and would be punished by the Dream people. He woke in his bed but no jewel was in his hand. The foster parents would not listen to his explanation and beat him savagely so that he was insensible for a long time.

When he revived it was mid-day and he got up and went out of the house and he decided to run away for ever.

He walked farther than he had ever walked before and he reached a barn, which was full of hay. It was now night and he slept in the barn and in his dreams he went to Dreamland where the people knew of his plight. They gave

35

him a gold coin and told him not to fear, and to walk to the far side of the Island where a kind family would look after him.

He set out next day and he walked very far before becoming hungry. He came to a small cottage and he asked the people in it for food and they gave him a big meal. He offered to pay with the gold coin. Though the people were poor, they were generous and they said that they could not change his gold coin but that if he ever returned that way, then he could pay them. He thanked the kind people and went on.

He was now very tired and he wondered if he was ever to reach the other side of the Island for the road went on and on and became steeper all the time. At last he reached the top of the mountain road and the way led downwards. Now it was easier and he walked faster and the mileposts passed more quickly.

He had not gone far down the mountain when a man with a horse and cart overtook him and he was told to climb into the cart. By the time the cart had to turn off the main road, Duncan had nearly reached the end of his journey.

In a green valley he saw the little cottage that the Dream People had shown him, and despite his tiredness he ran to it with all his strength.

A man and his wife were at the cottage waiting as if they had expected him. He asked if he could stay with them for he had run away from cruel foster parents and he had no one to go to.

Delight and amazement showed in the faces of the couple for they had no children and for many years they had prayed for a child; the night before they had dreamed that a child would come to them.

They told Duncan how glad they were to see him and they took him in by the fire and fed him and showed him how welcome he was.

He said that he would bring back jewels from Dreamland for them. 'See this ruby, it is a chip of Dreamland like a crystal ball but in the jewel you cannot see our world, only the things of Dreamland. I see the Dream People and sometimes I read stories of Dreamland in it. 'But the kind people said, 'Though we are poor, we have more than enough and we are happy. We asked only for a son and now that you have come, we shall never ask for anything again.'

Duncan knew in his heart that they spoke the truth and he was amazed for it was the first time in his life that people had wanted him and had thought him more important than the jewels of Dreamland.

He told his guardians of his adventures and how he went away as if his dreams were sailing ships which brought him to a wonderful world where we shall all meet one day and where all men are happy.

Days and weeks passed and his guardians were always kind to him and there was never any anger or hatred in the cottage. He kept asking if he could bring anything back from Dreamland for them to repay their kindness. But they told him they were happy to have him in the cottage and they gained so much joy from him that there was nothing else they wanted. They said that if he felt he must bring them something then let him bring a flower back from Dreamland.

So he went to the wonderful gardens of Dreamland and he chose the most lovely of the flowers. It was like a shimmering light and it had a fragrance that was sweeter than the sweetest earthly flowers.

The guardians took the flower and put it in a vase in their bedroom and the cottage was scented all day long, and they could not prevent themselves returning again and again to smell the flower and look at it. Next morning they rose after sleep and nothing was in the vase and when they looked closely, they saw a glimmer of colour and the faintest of scents. When they opened the window a wisp of rainbow coloured smoke vanished into the sky and they knew that the flower had returned to Dreamland.

The children of the village school were kind to Duncan for his guardians were well known in the village and they were greatly loved.

The years passed joyfully for the Dream Boy until a day came when the people of the town from which he had come learned where he was. The cruel foster parents had spent all the money that the jewels had brought and they were greedy for more.

The kindly guardians tried to keep the Dream Boy but they were told that the foster parents had the right to take him back. Sadly they said farewell to Duncan and told him that their house was his home and they would always have a welcome for him. Bitter tears came to the Dream Boy.

When he had returned to the house of his foster parents, he was told to bring back jewels as he used to do.

But when he went to Dreamland he could no longer find the treasury and when he looked for it everything became dark and he never again saw the jewels of Dreamland. The foster parents beat him unmercifully and only after many beatings did they realise that he could not bring them jewels any more. Now they treated him even more harshly for he was useless to them. At school the boys bullied him more cruelly than before and the Dream Boy felt despair. In the night he went to Dreamland and the people there felt sorry for him and they told him to run away again. They gave him gold coins and told him to leave on a ship and go away from the Island.

For many years no one in the town heard of him and no one cared. They thought that nothing good could come of him. But the kindly guardians thought of him often and they hoped and prayed that he would be well and that he would return safely to them. Many years passed and one of the men of the town who had known Duncan at school returned from a journey to London. He spoke to his friends, 'I was in the City when I saw an art gallery and a name on the outside of the building attracted my notice. It was the Dream Boy's. So out of curiosity I entered the gallery and looked at the pictures. The colours and shapes were weird and like nothing you have ever seen on this Earth. In walking round the gallery I came upon the Dream Boy and I hardly recognised him. I asked him if he still went to Dreamland and brought back jewels, and he replied, "I still go there but not to bring back jewels, only these dream pictures you see hanging on the walls".'

The Dream Boy was now famous and rich, but he was not happy. He knew that he had been driven too far away from men in his dreams and he had become one of the people of Dreamland. He had no friends here, only flatterers. One night he dreamed and he saw the kind guardians who had been his only real friends, and he knew his place was with them.

So he returned to the Island and the guardians were full of joy to see him again and they thought a miracle had happened and their hopes had come true.

Duncan remembered to repay the poor people who had fed him when he ran away from his foster parents.

He tried once to return to the town of his schooldays but as he approached it, a dark shadow fell across his thoughts and he felt sick and he had to turn back for the memories were too painful.

He hung his paintings on the walls of the cottage so that it was lit with the colours of Dreamland.

The guardians and the Dream Boy lived happily together all their lives, and Duncan knew that the compassion and love of his guardians were passports that took them across the frontiers of the dream world and let them meet him in the streets of Dreamland.

NICKY THE CLOCK

Long ago a craftsman was needed on the Isle of Man to mend all the broken things, and Nicky the Clock undertook to do this work. Although he could mend all sorts of metal things like clocks and toys, what he really liked mending were the dandelion clocks and the fuchsia bells when they went out of tune.

A notice was outside his house which proudly stated - 'Nicky the Clock - Mender of dandelion clocks and fuchsia bells'.

Nicky was not only a master craftsman but he was very proud of himself and he thought there was nothing he could not do. He mended the marble houses of the snails, and he patched the wings of butterflies so that in the autumn their frayed wings would let them fly away to the South with the swallows.

He dusted the wings of moths which were covered with the silver dust of the moonbeams. There was hardly anything he had not mended at some time for he was always looking for a challenge to his ingenuity.

He spliced the oars of the water boatmen. He was most proud of the splints he designed for a Daddy Long Legs that had broken a leg. It was said that after that Nicky was quite insufferable in his conceit for a time.

Nicky became interested in music and in the summer he was often to be seen in the meadows tuning the fiddles of the crickets and mending their bows. He even made a gargle for the choir of the frogs.

All these were quite easy problems for Nicky and it was not until he was confronted by the curlews that he was really tested.

At one time the curlews on the Isle of Man instead of piping their beautiful skirl were making a fearful noise and Nicky was called in to help.

First of all he studied all he could learn about the Curlew and he found that long ago a Scottish King had a wonderful singer in his Court who was also very beautiful and she had a husband who was the finest piper in Scotland. The trouble was that all the noblemen of the Court fell in love with the singer but she was faithful to her husband the piper and she repulsed all the advances of the suitors.

Because of the constant trouble in the Court, the King decided that the couple had to be banished so he told a sorcerer to rid him of the nuisance of the singer and her husband the piper.

The sorcerer changed the two of them into curlews who could live on the sea shore during the winter but in the summer they were banished to the moors.

On Scotland's sandy beaches they had no difficulty and the male curlew when he reached the moors and the glens piped as sweet a tune as the original piper. But it was different for the curlews of the Isle of Man, for the stops of their pipes became clogged with grit from the stony beaches and when the curlews reached the glens, they made a fearful noise.

One of the female curlews came to Nicky and complained for her mate no longer serenaded her. She said, 'There's nae skirl in the glens the noo'. She looked so sad and unhappy that Nicky felt he had to help. He soon showed the male curlews how to use the spikes of the reeds and the needles of the blackthorns to clean out their pipes.

So now those curlews are skirling more beautifully than ever. You can see the curlew pressing his wings against the bag of his body for he is a flying bagpipe, and he fills the glens with the wonder of his tune and his mate is always faithful to him the piper.

Nicky was prouder than ever and the notice outside his house now read - 'Nicky the Clock - Mender of clocks and toys and dandelion clocks and fuchsia bells and the fiddles of crickets and the pipes of curlews'.

After this Nicky felt his great abilities were not being fully used at all so he sought a far higher challenge that would really increase his stature.

In those days few doctors were on the Island and Nicky decided that he would try to help people with their sicknesses.

One day he called at a small home and he was told by two sorrowing parents that their daughter whose name was Edain had been ill for many months and nothing they could do helped her in any way.

Nicky looked at her and asked her many questions and after a long time he told her parents that he thought he knew what her trouble was. He said the girl had the most dangerous of all illnesses for she had lost her sweetheart and her heart was broken. He told them that he had never tried to mend a broken heart before but he was willing to try. Nicky spent many days in the house with the girl and he had the heart in a thousand little bits and pieces and he was trying very hard to put them all together again but some pieces seemed to be missing and some were broken and he had to take them home to his workshop to mend.

At last he had put all the pieces together except one which he could not find. Edain sat up smiling and happy and she immediately ran out of the house and went to see her friends. She was so happy and cheerful that everyone who saw her was amazed at what a change had been wrought by Nicky the Clock. But he was afraid because he knew that it could not last and he tried to find the missing part. He looked all over the Island, and he searched in every corner asking everyone he met if the part of the little girl's heart had been seen.

One day just as Nicky had feared, Edain stopped playing and her friends said they distinctly heard a whirring sound as of machinery inside her and she fell down and her friends had to carry her home.

Immediately Nicky was called and he came hurrying with his little box of tools but he still had no idea what to do to replace the missing part. He was terribly conscious of how important it was for him to succeed for he was conscientious and he hated to do shoddy work. He could see his reputation built up over many years being destroyed in a moment. People would say that Nicky was all very well when it came to fuchsia bells and dandelion clocks but don't ever ask him to mend a broken heart or anything important like that.

When Nicky arrived at the house of Edain, he found the girl in a fearful tangle - bits and wires and springs were all over the place. He started to put all the parts on a sheet of paper to make sure that none of the bits got away from him again.

But despite all his care and diligence, he found when he had assembled her heart again that another part was missing.

He was puzzled and worried and angry for he had taken every precaution. An idea came to him and he asked Edain's parents if they had any enemies and they told him that a mischievous imp had always delighted in playing tricks on them.

So Nicky went to the King of the Fairies who lived on South Barrule, for the Imps belong to the Fairies.

Nicky was given an audience and he told the King of the Fairies that an Imp had stolen parts of a little girl's heart and if he did not get them back, the poor little girl would never be well.

The King of the Fairies was sympathetic and said that he would do all he could to regain the parts that were missing. He sent out many of the fairies to make enquiries and he told them that they were not to return until the parts were found.

Nicky went back to the home of the little girl and he saw her playing with her friends but she was not cheerful and the other children said that sometimes she could not even remember her own name.

Nicky was now desperate and continued to look for the parts every waking moment of the day for he had no faith in the fairies finding the parts. He had been away for about two weeks when he got a call to return and take care of Edain whose heart had broken in pieces again.

Wearily Nicky took all the parts out once more and he had the parents beside the bed all the time to make sure that no one stole any more parts. They watched with the utmost care and they said at the end that no parts could possibly have been stolen.

And now Nicky put all the parts together again and when he had finished to his surprise no parts were missing any more, and Edain got up and she was the smiling Edain of old that her parents remembered and now she could play all the games of the children and never again did her heart break.

Now Nicky became prouder than ever and he put up an even larger notice outside his house saying that he had not only mended dandelion clocks and fuchsia bells and the fiddles of crickets and the bagpipes of curlews but now he could mend little girls' broken hearts as well.

LONAN AND TEEVAL

On the Isle of Man lived a young Prince named Orrie who was adventurous and he liked to climb mountains and scale cliffs. One day he was climbing the cliffs on Spanish Head when he noticed someone trapped at the foot of the precipice by the sea.

He climbed down and was just in time to rescue a young boy and carry him to safety before the incoming tide drowned him.

The boy whose name was Lonan revered the Prince from that day on till the end of his life. Lonan was the son of a poor farmer and the Prince saw that the young lad had spirit and courage beyond that of boys twice his age. They often talked about the myths of their Celtic ancestors and Orrie asked Lonan to go with him one day to find the Celtic City Numinor that sank beneath the waves.

Lonan remembered all his life how he swore to the Prince that he would help to find the City of the Sea.

When the Prince ascended the throne, Lonan was a young man and he became the Prince's bodyguard. Some men tried to kill the Prince and Lonan fought bravely at the side of the Prince and they routed the enemy.

The Prince showed his gratitude by promoting Lonan rapidly and in a few years he became the Captain of the Fleet. Despite his youth, Lonan soon defeated all the Prince's enemies.

The Prince now felt assured that his Kingdom was secure and it would be safe to go on the journey they had planned when they were boys.

They set out with their fleet and sailed to the North where they came upon lands of ice, but none of the men of the snow could tell them of the City Numinor.

They turned to the South and they sailed for many months and they came upon desert islands and lands of palms. One day they passed a coral island and the look out shouted that someone was at the edge of the sea. The Prince and Lonan entered a ship's boat and came near to the shore where a mermaid was sitting. She looked at them without fear and swam to their boat and she was taken to the ship.

The mermaid's name was Teeval and both the young men fell in love with her for she was beautiful. As the months passed they were able to speak with her for she had been quick to learn their speech.
Sometimes Lonan had the feeling that she knew what they were thinking long before any words were uttered.

The ships sailed fast for the wind was always fresh and they had no contrary winds or calms or storms. They sailed on month after month and they came forth from lands of ice and snow into a sea that seemed to have no end. Teeval asked them to sail their ships to the Kingdom where her Father lived, and they were glad to do so for neither Lonan nor the Prince knew where they were or where they were going.

The Prince thought he loved Teeval, but he was really scornful for he supposed her to be a simple and ignorant mermaid, who could never be a suitable bride for him. But Lonan thought she was the most wonderful woman he had ever seen, and he feared he was not worthy of her.

One day they were becalmed for the first time since Teeval had come on board. Round the ships were huge fish and whales and dolphins. Teeval called out to the creatures of the sea and they knew her for the dolphins swam close to the ship she was on and leaped out of the water. She spoke to them and hardly had she finished when they plunged beneath the waves and a few moments later the surface of the water was disturbed and a huge whirlpool appeared, and the sea became violently agitated. Fear came upon all the men of the fleet for they thought the ships would be sucked into the depths of the sea.

Teeval told the Prince not to be afraid and she urged him to swim with her into the vortex of the whirlpool for it was the way to her Father in the abyss of the sea.

But the Prince feared that he would be drawn down and be drowned for he did not trust Teeval who he supposed might be an evil magician. Instead he asked if any man in the fleet was brave enough to go with her into the whirlpool.

The sailors looked at the raging waters and not one of them had the courage except Lonan. Teeval took Lonan by the hand and she was glad for she preferred Lonan to the Prince. They jumped together into the sea and swam to the whirlpool and dolphins accompanied them into the depths.

Lonan felt himself going down and down and he could see Teeval beside him holding his hand and the dolphins guiding them. They reached crystal doors and entered a passageway that led to the Court of the Kings of the Ocean.

On a high throne sat Zal, King of the Ocean who was the Father of Teeval. She told the King that Lonan was the only man who had had the courage to descend with her into the Sea Kingdom.

King Zal looked at Lonan kindly and said it was well for nothing was more honoured among the men of the sea than courage. Lonan said he was the humble servant of the Prince who was brave, but it was not sensible for a Prince to risk his life needlessly.

King Zal said, 'It does my old ears good to hear your loyal speech. Now that you have seen that it is possible to come safely into the depths, go and

45

bring your Prince to us for we wish to see him and show him the hospitality of the sea.'

When Lonan had returned to the Courts of the Ocean, King Zal welcomed the Prince with courtesy and respect. The Prince looked about him and saw the jewels and the riches that were far beyond his dreams and an expression of avarice came upon his face and King Zal noticed it. But on the face of Lonan was only delight and openness and affection.

On the next day they set out to look at the Kingdom of the Ocean. The Prince was even more overwhelmed than on the previous day for the King of the Ocean ruled the wind and the waves; and all the myriad forms of life in the ocean paid homage to him . Here was more riches than in all the Kingdoms of the Land. A look of envy came on the face of the Prince and again King Zal saw it.

In contrast Lonan never thought of jewels and riches and his face was guileless and showed only pleasure. Lonan thought of noble things and at that moment he was thinking of the promise he had made to the Prince to look for the City Numinor that lay beneath the sea. And he supposed that the people of the Ocean would surely know of it. But even King Zal could tell him nothing of the City of the Sea.

They reached the far South and lands of perpetual ice. They entered caverns where the Ice Lords lived who were the allies of the King of the Ocean. But the Ice Lords had been driven from the caverns of ice, and now their enemies attacked the mermen. Lonan brought the King and the Prince to safety while he and the mermen fought the enemy. Lonan and the mermen were driven back by bloodless creatures of the ice who could not be harmed by steel or arrows.

Lonan forged fiery weapons and returned with the mermen to the caverns of ice and they hurled themselves on the enemy and drove them into the icy sea.

When Teeval learned how Lonan had saved her Father the King and his Prince, she knew that she loved him. He felt a delight and joy in being with her in the Kingdom of the Ocean and he wished never to return to the Land for he knew that he was really a merman and he had come home.

Unlike Lonan, the Prince who had not felt well since the day he descended to the Court of the Kings of the Ocean, became worse and Lonan knew that his Prince had to be brought to the surface of the sea or he would die.

When they reached the surface, the fleet was still waiting becalmed with the fish and dolphins and the whales playing round the ships.

A few days in the deep had changed the Prince and he was never to regain his former state. It was said of the Prince that from that time forward joy never came to him. The riches and the jewels and the power of the King of the

Ocean as well as the pressure of the depths had unbalanced his mind. Now he was jealous of Lonan, for the Prince had hoped to marry Teeval and become heir to the boundless riches of the Ocean, but now he knew that Teeval loved Lonan. The Prince thought with hatred and revulsion of the poor farm boy he had rescued from the sea and who he feared would become one of the great Princes of the World.

The Prince said farewell to Lonan but no warmth was in his words, only hatred. But Lonan's loyalty was too firm for him to notice his Prince's face. He bowed humbly and offered his service in whatever undertaking the Prince might want of him.

The months passed joyfully for Lonan beneath the sea and the mermen tested him and sent him on many expeditions so that he fought with all manner of creatures that were the enemies of the King of the Ocean. He remembered his promise to the Prince and on the expeditions he searched for Numinor the City of the Celts.

One day the dolphins who are the telegraphs of the Ocean and bring messages across the seas, told Lonan that the Prince needed help for his enemies were attacking the Isle of Man.

Teeval did not want Lonan to go for she had seen the looks of hatred on the face of the Prince and she had read his thoughts, and she feared for Lonan. But King Zal said Lonan must go for a man must match his deeds with his words, "Had not Lonan promised to help the Prince whenever help was needed?'

Lonan took with him his faithful mermen who had followed him in the battles of the sea. They went in the fleet of the Ocean and with them went the legions of the sea - the dolphins and the whales and the sharks and the cuttle-fish. This force reached the Island just as the enemy were landing and were about to attack the army of the Prince. The creatures of the sea caused such waves that the enemy ships were scattered. Half the enemy force had already landed and the Prince's soldiers were fleeing the field of battle when Lonan and his mermen fell upon the Vikings and drove them into the sea.

The Prince saw the marvellous power of the King of the Ocean that Lonan commanded and he felt humiliated that his boyhood friend had now so much more power than he had. He sensed that Lonan had become one of the Great Ones of the Earth, and his jealousy increased. At the banquet in celebration of victory, Lonan said that he had been instructed that if they were victorious and saved the Isle of Man, he should ask the Prince for a dowry. Without the dowry, Lonan said he could not marry Teeval, the Princess of the Ocean.

The Prince said he would send the dowry but he was even more jealous because the loss of Teeval still stung. The Prince's face went white and it was as if he went mad for he ordered that the food of Lonan be poisoned.

But the mermen knew the thought of the Prince and when the poisoned dish was brought one of them stood up and pretended to stumble and struck the dish from the servant's hand. He apologised for his clumsiness, and sat down. The Prince said nothing but he sensed that Lonan was protected by magic powers.

Such was Lonan's loyalty that he would not believe that the Prince had tried to poison him. Even when he was told that one of the dogs of the palace had died after eating the food, he still did not believe it.

Lonan and the victorious mermen returned to the Court of the King of the Ocean and for many months Lonan waited for the dowry to come, but at last word came that the Prince would not send it.

So Lonan went to King Zal and said that he no longer expected the money and though he loved Teeval he had no hope of winning her. He added that the Prince his friend must have had bad harvests otherwise he would surely have sent the dowry that had been promised.

King Zal said, 'I am astonished by your loyalty for I have never seen its like in all the regions of the Ocean. Your Prince is more prosperous than he has ever been for I sent vast shoals of fish and multitudes of crabs and scallops to swell his harvest of the sea.'

He paused and then continued, 'Concern yourself no longer with the dowry. What would we, the People of the Sea do with a dowry from the Prince of a small island when our riches are as boundless as the Ocean? I made it a condition only so that I might test you and your Prince.'

King Zal smiled at Lonan and said, 'By your loyalty to us and to your Prince and the brave service you have rendered us, you have won all our hearts and I command that the preparations for your marriage to Princess Teeval be made without delay.'

After their marriage, Teeval and Lonan went to the far islands of the ocean. Teeval told him how the atolls were not part of the land but of the sea for it was her own subjects of the sea who had spun the salt and the spray and the air and the water into those jewels of the ocean more lovely than the oases of the deserts. Teeval's handmaidens had helped her set the green jewels of the atolls across the floor of the ocean.

After the long years of service and warfare, Lonan enjoyed the ease of life with Teeval playing in the blue fields of the ocean. But a day came when King Zal became too old to rule and Teeval was crowned Queen of the Ocean. New powers descended on her and a sense of awe came upon the creatures of the sea when they saw her. Even the waves became submissive which had formerly been playful and wayward.

The Land of Teeval is for ever on the horizon. If men approach in friendliness they may be made welcome but if not, her lands recede so that men never reach the region of the Queen of the Ocean for it is like the end of the rainbow that no man finds. For her the waves sing and dance. No men go lightly into the mighty ocean or enter it proudly for Teeval will destroy them and their puny ships.

There was no more rest for Lonan and he went from one end of her domains to the other fighting her enemies and at last he conquered all of them for her.

It was then that a message came by the dolphins that the Prince had asked Lonan to come to him for the Vikings had ravaged his lands again and starvation was facing his people.

Teeval became angry for she did not want her husband who was the Admiral of all the forces of the Ocean to be taken away to fight the little battles of the Isle of Man, when he was needed for the wars of the Ocean. She told Lonan that the Prince hated him and this time would surely kill him.

But Lonan said that her enemies were no more and he would soon return after settling the troubles of the Isle of Man. He said that he had sworn to help the Prince and he would do so as long as the Prince still lived.

Nothing Teeval said could change his resolve so he set out with his brave mermen in only one ship for he thought it wrong to take Teeval's navy away from her in a war of which she did not approve. When he reached the Island, the Prince told Lonan that he must attack the stronghold of the enemy in the Northern Lands alone for the Island could not spare any ships or men.

Lonan said he could not defeat the Vikings with a single ship and his few soldiers. But the Prince cared less for the defeat of the enemy than to see his old subordinate humbled and killed so he ordered Lonan to go as he was.

Lonan knew that he and his brave men would be killed yet so great was his loyalty that he bowed to the command of the Prince. The Prince gloated when he saw the single ship departing towards the North, for he knew he would at last be rid of the man who was loved on the Island and had become the hero of all the people.

When Lonan arrived at the enemy's coast he was set upon by overwhelming numbers of ships. Though he and his men fought bravely they were on the point of defeat when suddenly a storm arose and the enemy ships were thrown against the cliffs and many of the ships were overturned. Lonan thanked the sea for his deliverance, and then the dolphins appeared and he was told that it was Teeval who had followed him and had come to his rescue.

Lonan took the ships of the enemy that had not been sunk and using his men as crew he sailed them to the Isle of Man. The Prince was waiting for news of Lonan's death and when the first ships were seen, he supposed that it was the Viking fleet that had defeated Lonan.

When Lonan entered Peel Harbour, he found the Prince's army drawn up to fight. As soon as the Prince saw that it was Lonan with the captured fleet he was astonished and dismayed and he vowed that he would kill Lonan that very night.

When all the people in the palace were sleeping. Lonan awoke to the noise of fighting. He took his sword and ran towards the sound of the fighting.

The Prince was being attacked by his own guards who had mutinied and were intent on killing him. Lonan rushed to the aid of the Prince and the two of them were able to fight off the great numbers of the guards. When Lonan had made the last of the guards flee, he turned to the Prince who sank to the floor. Lonan dropped his sword and supported the Prince in his arms. The Prince shook his head and said he was wounded and would die. He turned to Lonan and with a look of sorrow on his face he asked forgiveness for trying to kill Lonan and for wronging him who had been the loyalest and the best man he had ever had in his service.

Lonan forgave him gladly and said, "Nothing needs to be forgiven for all I am is due to you. You saved my life as a boy and ever after I thought of my life as forfeit to you to do with as you chose. If it had not been for you, I should be a poor soldier in the Army, but you made me the Captain of your fleet and now I am the Consort of the Queen of the Ocean. All I feel is gratitude for you. If you ever had a fault it came not from yourself but from the injury you suffered in the depths of the sea.'

The Prince's face lighted up at Lonan's words and tears came to his eyes and the madness left him. He regained his affection for his old boyhood friend and he was contented.

Lonan stayed to see the crowning of the Prince's son on the throne of Man and he returned to the Kingdom of the Ocean.

He and Teeval were happy all their days and when he was not helping her rule the Kingdom, he wandered like the Celts who have peopled the Islands of the ocean, journeying but never knowing what they sought. But Lonan knew what he sought and it was Numinor the City of the Sea. And Lonan thought always with veneration and love of his Prince whose vision of Numinor had made Lonan what he was, for men are made great by the greatness of the vision that inspires them.

51

MANANNAN ISLE

It was mid-summer and Gareth had just risen and gone down to the beach at Port Erin. A strange craft was in the harbour. It was wide and had a furled sail, which had unusual markings on it. No one was there except a sailor who by his appearance Gareth supposed must have been in charge of the craft.

Gareth marvelled at people who would arrive from the ocean in a boat that was not sea worthy. He sensed something mysterious about the boat and the sinister sailor on the end of the pier.

In the night he had seen in a dream that he would experience a day of wonder. Still pondering he walked along the road beside the beach and climbed the steep hill to the shops. A woman came towards him. She was young and beautiful and when her eyes looked at him, he felt fear and apprehension for a power was in her glance that forced him to go to her. He sensed compulsion as if she had drugged him or cast a spell over him. The world around him blurred and he felt far away and he heard a voice which must have been his own saying, 'You are a stranger here, may I guide you while you are in our town?'

He felt he was struggling to wake from a dream in which he had reached the depths of the sea.

She nodded her head and told him her name was Itara. He would have told her his name but his mind could remember nothing. His memory had left him and he could think only of the woman who was beside him. He knew that she was not a woman of the Earth but a magical woman who might vanish into the air.

His mind cleared and his fear slowly left him and the day brightened into one of enchantment, and every moment passed like a dream. All things about him seemed unreal and they were like pictures and even the clouds were great ships floating on the palest of seas with their billowing sails shining. Itara had led him into an enchanted world where all things were bright and full of colour. Nothing was drab or mean or earth coloured for everything shone with the colours of the sky and the grass and the sunset and the rainbow.

The hours went by in delight and the sleepy town began to awake and the bustle of the day started but for Gareth other people were as visions and he recognised no one, yet many who passed by him were his friends. People noticed the expression of wonder on his face and they saw the beautiful woman beside him, and they marvelled at him and some feared for him. Gareth led Itara away from the town and they swam in the sea and Gareth saw that Itara swam like no creature of the land but like a dweller of the deep so graceful and swift she was in the water. And Gareth wondered the more.

All day long they were together and each time she touched him it was as if a current of power passed through him and he was more enchanted than before and more full of wonder and delight.

He heard her say that they would meet only this one time and they could never meet again for she lived in a land where no man could follow her. The evening was drawing on and it was approaching the time when Itara had to leave him. He felt sorrow and loneliness that he was never to see her again. He asked where she lived so that he might go to her in his boat for he was a sailor.

She said nothing but he saw a vision of an enchanted kingdom and he knew it was the place where Itara lived. And he saw that no boat could ever reach there.

She kissed him but he had so much sadness that he felt no joy in the love she bore him.

He asked why he could not come with her in the boat that had brought her. He saw a look of hope on her face but it immediately left her and she said, 'They will never let you come and even if you do come it will be the end for you. We are of a different world and there can be no lasting meeting between your people and mine.'

He scarcely heard what she said for he still saw the vision of the land where Itara lived and he looked at it through her eyes. He saw a people of the Sea and he knew that Itara was sad and lonely there and wanted him to come with her. So he spoke to the ten people who were already in the boat, and asked permission to come with her.

They looked with astonishment at one another and then the leader rose and said, 'No! You cannot come with us.'

'Is it because you have no room in the boat?'

'We have room in the boat but we go where no men have ever gone before.'

Gareth who was young and strong became angry and he jumped into the boat and took up his position beside Itara.

The Leader said to him, 'There are many things you do not know. If you come with us you will never return to the world of men.'

'I am tired of life here and I shall be happier with Itara even if I never return.'

The Leader once more spoke to Gareth. 'You are stubborn and foolish. Listen to a man older and wiser than you. If you come with us you will never see your friends again and your body will not be able to live in our land and you will never win Itara. It is very sure you will be unhappy. Now leave us and give us no more trouble.'

But Gareth was defiant, 'If you want me to leave you must throw me ashore by force, I will not leave her.'

The Leader looked at Gareth pityingly and nodded to the sailors to cast off and

53

hoist sail. He said, 'I have warned you but you are too foolish to listen.'

The craft went swiftly for the breeze was stiff and soon they came out of the Bay and they saw the Calf of Man. They kept clear of Kitterland and made for the South of the Calf. After some hours of sailing, in which time it became dark, they reached the end of the Calf and were passing Chicken Rock. To Gareth's surprise he saw lights in the distance to the South where he had never seen lights before. Soon they could hear singing and music and the sound of revelry. The boat came to a harbour on a small island that was glittering with lights and many people were dancing and their bright clothing made a joyful scene. He saw no old people and even the leader of the boat who Gareth had supposed to be old was really young.

Itara took Gareth by the hand and ran with him to the festival. There were booths such as are seen at fun fairs, and there was drink, which made men light of heart. Gareth felt extreme joy as he walked with Itara for he was still under the spell she had woven and he thought he was in wonderland.

The festivities went on for a long time but it was now nearing midnight and suddenly all the people stopped dancing and they stood holding hands and they sang a song of farewell that was very sad and heart rending. All the people were looking in the direction of the Isle of Man to which they showed a warm affection for it was their ancestral home.

A bell sounded and the people turned and entered a passageway that led into the Island. They reached a huge hall with large windows in the ceiling through which they saw the stars. A clock struck midnight and soon after they felt a sensation of descending. Waves splashed on the windows above Gareth's head and he could see fish and seaweed. Soon it grew dark as the outside lights dimmed and the interior lights came on and an undersea kingdom was disclosed. At that moment a feeling of dread came over him and he was afraid and Itara took his arm and the energy from her revived him but soon he was more tired than he had ever been and he said he had to rest.

He had many dreams during the night and more fears came to him. He saw Itara not as a lover but as an enticer who had taken him away from the Isle of Man by witchcraft and she did not love him at all.

He woke feeling ill and the joy of the previous day had left him and he felt fear and discouragement. He was still tired as he was led by a guide through passages of crystal. They went past gardens of sea flowers; crystals grew there like flowers on the land. Coloured sea weeds were the brilliant foliage of the sea gardens, and filaments of metal that had the most brilliant colours he had ever seen sparkled like ice crystals. The gardens were lit by self luminous animals of the sea and the water itself was irridescent and shone from particles of gold light floating in it. His mind felt dull and he did not warm to the beauty of the gardens.

He was brought into the Court of the Leader of the Island who Gareth learned was a puppet; for the Isle of Manannan was a small outpost of the lands of the Sea, ruled by Manannan the Great King of the Sea. In front of Gareth was a man sitting on a throne decorated with creatures of the Sea.

A voice boomed out from the throne, 'Young man, in spite of being told you were not welcome, you forced your way on to the Island. If you had understood that you would not be able to leave us for many years you might have been less impetuous. This Island of Manannan rises to the surface of the sea for one day only in every seven years.

'You have also had the folly to fall in love with one of our women. This is especially so for she is promised to the Great Lord of the Southern Ocean. She did wrong even to speak to you. If you wish to see the Isle of Man ever again, you will have nothing more to do with her and you will never look at her again.'

'You will work in the workshops lest you gain a habit of idleness in the time that you must remain with us.'

Gareth had no time to speak for the Leader who was a small minded and fearful person, intolerant of thoughts different from his own, left the hall abruptly and Gareth was led away.

The joy and wonder that he felt with Itara had ended and the sickness from the pressure of the depths increased and he felt faint and dizzy. His life became dull and only in dreaming did he see things to cheer him. In his dreams he saw Itara clearly as if she was in the flesh during the day he spent with her at Port Erin. But when he woke he knew only the sadness of being parted from her and yet the idea that she still loved him persisted and gave him hope.

A day came for a festival and all the people went to the Hall of Assembly. Gareth looked for Itara amongst the huge throng and he saw her at the side of the room looking down dejectedly. When he went to her and took her hands he felt the same feeling of power that he had always felt but her face when it looked up into his was sad. He was struck with dismay at how much she had changed for she looked old and sick.

She told him that they must never meet for her future husband, the Lord of the Southern Ocean was very jealous and would kill them both if they persisted in their love. She asked him to leave her and he saw tears in her eyes.

The days passed even slower for Gareth and he wondered if he would survive the Island of Manannan for his will to live without Itara had weakened and his sickness increased.

He forced himself to go to work each day and one of the artisans called Agon helped Gareth and they often spoke together after work. They gained an affection for one another and Agon began to regard Gareth as his son. Gareth learned that the Lord of the Southern Ocean whom Itara was to marry, though young like all the people of the Sea, was really very old and he was not a suitable match for her. Agon said that she was very unhappy but it was the law of the people of the Sea that parents could make a daughter marry whom they chose. Her parents would gain importance and riches if she married the Southern Lord; whereas if she married a stranger who was not even of the Sea at all, she would be dishonoured and her parents would be disgraced. The timid Leader of the Island feared Manannan might become angry even at a stranger being in his lands.

The people of the Island watched Itara and Gareth weakening and they feared for the life of Itara. Even the healing strength of Manannan did nothing for her and the physicians lost hope. Agon pleaded for Itara and Gareth but the Leader had so much fear and meanness and hardness in his heart that he would not let them meet even at the cost of her life.

Agon became angry and he determined to help Itara. He was not only an incomparable workman in metals but he knew all the passages of the Island and he was familiar with the deepest mines where the Islanders formerly mined gold and precious stones.

When the day came for Itara to leave the Island and go to the Southern Ocean to marry, no one could find her. The people searched day after day but they found no sign of her. It was thought that she had drowned by going through one of the undersea hatches.

In the days that followed Gareth looked even sadder than ever. When the search had been abandoned and all the people were asleep Agon led Gareth into dark mines below the Island. They went through many passages and made so many turns that Gareth could not remember the way but at last they reached a cell behind a hidden door where Itara was waiting.

As soon as she saw Gareth she sat up and a smile came to her face but she looked so ill that Gareth feared she would die. They talked of escaping together and leaving the Island when it next rose to the surface of the sea, and with that hope to strengthen her, she said she would survive and already she looked better and some colour came to her cheeks.

They could not see each other often for each time they met they risked their lives and the life of Agon who was also in danger. As the years passed, Itara recovered from her sickness and despite living in a dungeon-like room she was happy. Gareth also recovered but he took care to look as ill as he formerly did.

At last it came time for Gareth to leave for the seven years were nearly ended and it was approaching mid summer.

Gareth often wondered how Agon would arrange the escape of Itara. Agon built a large sea chest whose purpose he said was to hold all the metal work Gareth had made during his stay on the Island, which would be valuable to him when he returned to the Isle of Man.

The Islanders who saw the chest were suspicious and Gareth knew that if Itara were hidden in it the Islanders would certainly open it and find her.

The day for leaving came and as the Island was rising, Gareth and Agon brought the chest to the entrance of the passage that led to the surface of the Island. They opened the chest and with a gathering of suspicious people around them including the Leader of the Island, they filled the empty chest with Gareth's work and the chest was locked and the key given to Gareth.

The Island reached the surface of the sea and people rushed to get to the top of the Island.

Agon sent Gareth ahead while he arranged the carrying of the chest to the boat. It seemed to Gareth that he had been in the boat only for a few moments when Agon arrived with the chest which was put in the bottom of the boat.

Agon embraced Gareth as a son and wished him well. Gareth felt numb and cold from disappointment because Agon had failed him after all for it was the same chest.

The sea was calm for the Islanders always chose a fine day for the raising of the island. Port Erin was reached and Gareth carried the chest ashore and bade the Islanders farewell. He struggled with the heavy chest and found lodgings and no sooner had he closed the door of the room than he heard a muffled voice from within the chest. He quickly opened it and inside was Itara.

She told him that Agon was the greatest magician of all the lands of the Sea and for him the feat was easy. She told him how they had exchanged the chest with another one that Agon had put nearby and no one had noticed in the excitement of the surfacing of the Island.

They were so happy together that they could not believe that life could be so wonderful. But after the first year had ended they became poor for the money from the sale of the articles of work that Itara had been able to bring with her in the chest had all been sold and Gareth found no work on the Island, so they suffered hunger and destitution.

With sadness he told her that men of the Isle of Man since the beginning of history had to be ready to leave to earn money abroad.
She feared what he said but despite feeling ill away from Manannan
Isle, she knew that he had to leave her.

Gareth left her in the care of Kathryn a friend who had helped them in the past. The years passed and Gareth returned to her on leaves and he sent money so that she had enough to eat but she missed Gareth and the days were sad and lonely. Not only did she miss Gareth and her childhood home, she now knew something more terrible. The people of the Isle of Manannan cannot live very long on the land and each year of time on the land aged her seven years and already she had become old.

She looked in the mirror and she wondered if Gareth still loved her after his last visit.

Then no money came from Gareth and he returned to her no more, and Itara had to go hungry often though the faithful Kathryn still helped as much as possible but this was less than formerly for hardship had come to all the people of the Isle of Man.

More years passed and Itara had become older still and her eyes were dull and sunken in her head and her face was wrinkled and her hair had turned grey. So old had she become that she wondered if she would live long enough to be able to go on the boat when it arrived from Manannan Isle. She felt her limbs and they were like sticks and she knew that she would not even be able to reach the boat without help.

Only weeks remained until midsummer and the boat from Manannan Isle would be in the harbour. Kathryn feared for her friend and she suspected that Gareth had seen Itara's ugliness and had become ashamed and had found another woman in a distant land. Sorrow was in the house and no laughter was heard and the days passed slowly.

On the morning when the boat from Manannan Isle arrived they had heard no word of Gareth, and Itara thought that she had been deserted, and yet she could not quite believe it and she still hoped and prayed. It was towards evening when a small sailing boat was seen to come into the Bay and Kathryn went to the harbour without hope. The lone sailor in the boat was Gareth and Kathryn ran to him and told him of Itara and how he must take her quickly to Manannan Isle or she would die.

Gareth hardly recognised Itara. He told her that at first he had been successful as a sailor but on the last voyage he had been shipwrecked and he was the only survivor. He had passed years on a deserted island until he made himself a raft and reached habited land.

Though he was shocked by her ugliness he had learned that it was not the appearance that mattered but the gold of the heart so he lifted her into his arms and carried her proudly to the harbour. Hideous though she was he had no remorse, only sadness for he still loved her.

When the people of Manannan Isle saw Itara they had compassion for her and she was laid in the bottom of the boat and they tried to feed her but she could not eat so weak had she become.

Even when they reached Manannan Isle she did not recover and Gareth thought he had returned too late. The Physicians also held out no hope for her. Only Agon said that if she was brought to Manannan quickly she might yet be saved.

So Gareth took her by the great highways of the Sea to the Courts of the Kings of the Sea. When they were still far away they detected an increase of light in the crystal passages of the Sea, and the highways became wider and the sentinels more numerous. Great fish were the beacons of those highways of the Lords of the Sea.

They passed immense portals of crystals set with precious jewels of the Sea. They knew they were at last in the Court of the Kings of the Sea. Far away in a brilliant cloud of light they saw a being who shone with blue light. Gareth cast his hands over his face for the glare hurt his eyes.

Beings that looked pale like the water were round the throne and Gareth could discern them one by one approaching the seated King whose hand when it touched them, healed for they turned into bright beings that shone with flashing light.

And now Gareth neared the throne and he recognised some of the pale beings that had become exhausted in Manannan's service and had come to be made whole. Manannan was as a fountain of power and healing. Gareth felt fear in the Great Court of the King of the Sea for he and Itara had done wrong to escape from Manannan Isle. He thought that instead of healing her, Manannan would destroy them both for he had a look of implacable strength and resolve on his face.

Gareth lifted Itara high in his arms like a child and called to Manannan to have mercy on them. He went forward with Itara in his arms and Manannan fixed his eyes upon her and it seemed to Gareth that a look of compassion crossed his face and he stretched out his hand and touched Itara on the cheek.

Gareth stepped back and carried Itara away and he felt extreme sorrow for no change came over her and he feared that Manannan had refused to save her. But just as he left the Court, he saw a flicker of flame play across the face of Itara and within minutes she had changed and her hair turned golden, and her face and body became as young as when he first met her. Now she was able to stand and Gareth felt her strength surge through him as it used to do.

When they reached Manannan Isle they were welcomed joyfully for the Lord of the Sea had sent a message that he had pardoned them. And now Gareth felt the wonder and delight of his first meeting with Itara long ago for the world changed and it was as if he was bewitched and all the people looked happy and joy filled his days.

Every seven years they visited their faithful friend Kathryn and brought her priceless gifts from the Sea. Their friend Agon was made the Leader of Manannan Isle and happiness filled all the people for Agon led them to prosperity and the arts were revived and contentment came to all the people of Manannan Isle.

THE TARROO UISHTAI

A little girl lived in a house where two rivers met near the sea. Her name was Rhoda and she was very lonely for she had no brothers or sisters and she rarely saw her Father who was always away from home, and her Mother was a hard hearted woman who had no love for Rhoda. Rhoda learned to make friends of the animals who all loved her for she was gentle and kind.

She liked to walk beside the stream and she often followed it to the Sea. Sometimes she thought she saw something in the shadows cast by the trees but always when she reached the place she found nothing. The stream was the haunt of a young tarroo uishtai who often saw Rhoda but he hid from her for he knew that she would be frightened if she saw him.

A tarroo uishtai, although its name means water bull, is really more like a dolphin than a land bull and it is a wise animal. He used to follow Rhoda and though she never saw him, he was always close to her. One day it chanced that she was climbing among the rocks and cliffs at the edge of the Sea and suddenly she lost her footing and fell and she was swept into the deep water. She cried for help but she knew that no one could save her. When she had given up hope, she felt herself being lifted out of the water on a broad back; and she heard a gentle voice coming from a huge creature telling her to cling to his horns. Very quickly the tarroo uishtai rescued her from the water and took her to her home.

She was very grateful and wondered how she could ever repay him for his kindness. But the tarroo uishtai said it was not always necessary to repay every kindness and anyway she had always been kind to all the other animals and she could think of her rescue as repayment to her. When she understood what he said she sensed that the tarroo uishtai was gentle and kinder than men.

Almost every day she used to go to the stream in quest of the tarroo uishtai and he became her closest friend for he was more understanding than the other animals and birds. The two of them would roam on the seashore and she would go on his back into the deep sea and she was never afraid when she was with the tarroo uishtai for he was strong and not even the most terrible storms could frighten him.

As the years passed, Rhoda grew into a young woman and the tarroo uishtai became stronger and swifter. He was like a horse but of matchless swiftness and he could swim in the sea like a dolphin. She grew to love the tarroo uishtai as young girls learn to love the horses they ride. She groomed his sleek sides and plaited his hair over his forehead. These were the happiest days of Rhoda's life and each day she was carried into the sea and they played amidst the waves of the sea with the sea creatures that were their friends.

As time went on it seemed to Rhoda that an unfathomed sadness was in the eyes of the tarroo uishtai and she knew that it was because he thought she would leave him. So she told him that they had been friends all her life and he had saved her, and she could never leave him. But he said it was the old story of friendships between men and tarroo uishtais that human beings would always leave for they were not as faithful as tarroo uishtais. He said to her, 'You think you will always be with me, but there are things over which you have no power, and soon you will leave me and not because you are forced but of your own free will.'

Rhoda laughed and said he was talking nonsense and she would never leave him and certainly not of her own accord.

A time came when Rhoda's parents resented the food that Rhoda ate and the cost of keeping her and they decided that she must marry and be sent away.

Many suitors came to Rhoda but she refused them and she told each one of them that she wanted to stay by her home near the sea. And her Mother guessed that something was preventing her daughter from leaving so she followed Rhoda down to the sea and saw the great tarroo uishtai and Rhoda riding on its back in the sea.

Her Mother and Father spoke angrily together and it was decided that they would have one more party at which all the young men of the neighbourhood would be invited and she would have to decide on one of the young men. If she did not choose one of them she would be sent away from home and face destitution.

At the party Rhoda's eye fell on one of the handsomest men she had ever seen and in a moment she had forgotten the tarroo uishtai and she fell in love with the young man.

Throughout the party the two young people were together and they danced and laughed and Rhoda felt happy.

When the party ended and all the guests had left and Rhoda was alone she went down to the stream and suddenly she remembered the tarroo uishtai. Beside the stream were splashes of water and she knew at once that it was not water splashing from the stream but the tears of the tarroo uishtai. The tears led down to the sea to a pool of tears where he had waited long, looking back for her, and she knew that he had gone for ever, and a terrible sadness and dread came over her.

It was not long afterwards that Rhoda was married and it soon came out that her husband's handsome face hid a cruel and mean nature. She now lived in a hard part of the Island with no stream and the sea was far away and she had only rocks and wind and cold. No love was in her home and she worked long hours and she felt only the scorn and hatred of her husband and the lack of kindness and love. Long years of unhappiness were the lot of Rhoda.

One day she asked her husband to let her return to her parents for a few days because her Father was now very old and she wanted to see him while he was still hale. Her husband let her go with a curse. When she saw the stream of her childhood again she bitterly regretted marrying and leaving. She went sadly down to the sea and called for the tarroo uishtai but the waves gave no answer, and the birds of the sea shore said they had never again seen him, and they had found no sign of him not even the tears on the shore. And the gulls' cries of sorrow told her that he had gone for ever.

She went down to the shore again in the morning as soon as the sun had risen and she called and called, and far in the distance she heard his voice and she ran into the sea and let herself be carried on the currents.

Never again was Rhoda seen by the two rivers but she is happy for she has gone to the land of the tarroo uishtais which is at the end of the ocean. And yet she comes back with the tarroo uishtai to the place of the two rivers, and they play on the sea shore, but no men see them. Only sometimes during storms amidst the white horses, a figure is seen clinging to the back of a dark creature. And sometimes tears are seen on the sand beside the sea, and in the coves are the snortings of the tarroo uishtai.

SEERESS OF THE TREES

An orphan boy named Ewan had lived a happy life with his Mother and Father but when he was eight they both died and he was sent to foster parents who resented him. The foster parents were unkind to him and always favoured their own children. Ewan was treated cruelly and harshly and he was given less food than the other children got and he had to work long hours for nothing. He was used as a servant in the house and there was no play for Ewan for the other children learned to treat him as a servant and never to play with him.

One day in the week he was freed from his ill treatment for his foster parents thought they were religious and allowed no work on Sundays. On that day only, Ewan was allowed to do what he liked and he used to go far away in the mountains where he made friends with the animals and the birds. Though he had too little food himself he always had enough so that in winter when his friends were hungry he could bring them a little food.

One day he walked through a steep valley where he had never gone before and he struggled through thick undergrowth and he had to climb across a gorge where the stream narrowed between two precipices. The gorge was long but eventually opened out into a green valley of fair trees and a lush meadow. It was a sheltered place which the sun reached all day long. Affer his climb in the gorge he was exceedingly weary and he lay down under a great Oak tree that was the largest tree in the valley. The animals had followed him and the birds put leaves and moss over him so that a wonderful quilt covered him and kept him warm while he slept.

In sleep a dream came to him. It was as if he was taken back to a time when huge creatures were on the earth. Giants and Giantesses walked the land and farmed it and hunted in the mountains. Other creatures were the enemies of the Giants, and they were black and far bigger than the giants - great hulks with teeth like tusks of mammoths. These creatures were ogres that always attacked the giants and both sides formed armies and battles were waged on the mountain sides where the ogres lived.

The war went on generation after generation and sometimes the ogres gained and sometimes the giants. But the God of the Island, Manannan became more and more angry for he did not like war in his domains and the giants and the ogres waged perpetual war. Although he threatened the ogres, they never listened for they loved warfare too much. The giants would have liked to stop fighting but they were forced to defend themselves. At last Manannan's patience wore out and he cursed the Ogres and cast a spell on them so that if they ever came out of their mountain caves and saw the sun they would be

turned to stone. And now they can still be seen on the sides of the mountains where they were frozen into rocks. And Manannan also cursed the Giants but since their guilt was not so great as the guilt of the Ogres, he did not turn them into rocks. Instead he caused them to be rooted to the Earth so they could not move and attack the ogres ever again. Yet there is life in the rock hearts of the ogres for they still seek to do harm to the Giants that have become trees. And the trees also continue to fight but the war between the two sides is so slow that no one can notice it any more. But through the years the trees sometimes advance up the valleys into the mountains but they never reach the peaks for the trees are thrown back by the ogres from their fastnesses in the high mountains. And sometimes the rock Ogres are seen to hurl themselves down the sides of the mountains as they used to do long ago but the trees rally despite the injuries done to them and they return to overcome the Ogres.

Though the Giants were turned into trees, they still remember their long history and all the knowledge that they had learnt in their millions of years on the Earth. The trees can no longer move but they can think and the great tree under which Ewan was sleeping was the story teller oak for she had been a Seeress of the Giants.

She felt sorrow for the poor, thin orphan boy who lay at her feet and she wanted to help him by teaching him the knowledge of the trees. First she taught him the history of the trees on the Island and how the Ayres were formed by the hand of the sculptors of the ice, and how the trees of the Island had been destroyed by the ice but the truth that they knew had been saved in their sleeping young and the trees of the far South. She taught how men came generation after generation and cut down the trees and burned them so that few were left on the Island.

Now the first lesson had ended for it was late and Ewan woke up and he found his head ached and he was bewildered by all the knowledge he had learned for in sleep the mind can learn more things than when it is awake. He hurried home and he was chided and beaten for returning late. The days of the week passed with his foster parents treating him cruelly but now he was less sad for he had a friend in the great tree, and he had always something to look forward to on Sundays. Each time he slept under the Great tree he learned many new things. He was taught how the gnarled bark of the trees is only a shield and within is a spirit who can escape in sleep and be free in the glades of the forest. He was told the long and tragic history of the trees and when he woke the trees round him were shedding tears for they also listened to the sad story. They showed him drops of amber which were the tears of an ancient forest that had been killed long ago.

He learned the strange language of the trees and was taught the lore of all the animals and birds that lived in the forest. He mastered the properties of the plants so that he could cure human sickness.

When he slept under the tree, he not only gained wisdom but he was given strength and courage that came from the great heart of the tree.

Now when he was at home, he would sometimes tell his foster parents things which they did not know and which no men knew. But Ewan's knowledge made his wicked and jealous foster parents hate him more for he showed himself to be cleverer than his foster brothers though he never went to school

As the years passed, he became calm and tranquil and in his dealings with men and even his foster parents he returned kindness for evil just as the great tree had taught him to do, and all who knew him said that he was no ordinary boy but one of the wise ones.

It troubled him nonetheless that though he learned the teachings of the trees he never learned the teachings of men which would be needed if he was to make his way in the world.

The Old tree said to him, 'You will learn from me the greatest things, things that men always forget though they are what the Prophets tell them generation after generation. We trees are the haven for all things. Our boughs are the homes of birds and squirrels and the holes in our trunks are the homes of the owls and the little birds. The mice and the rabbits live amongst our roots. From us you will learn to love all things and to hate none. We give shade even to the one who cuts off our branches."

Nevertheless the Old tree told him to go to the lady who lived in the valley near the waterfall at the foot of the gorge. She would teach him the learning of men for she had been a teacher.

So now Ewan learned from the old Oak and the lady in the valley.

Time passed and Ewan gained in wisdom and at last he became a man but no work was to be found on the Island so he had to go to sea.

The Captain of the ship on which he had embarked was a kindly man who found Ewan to be bright and willing. At first Ewan was only the cabin boy but the Captain helped him and soon Ewan was given larger responsibilities for the Captain could see that he had found a fine sailor and one able to take on any work however difficult. It was not many years before Ewan had become first mate on the ship and because he treated men in the way the great tree had taught him, he was greatly loved and respected and the ship's crew were the happiest in the fleet.

Time went on and he became Captain of the ship and he was able to trade on his own account and he became rich and all the sailors with him prospered in his service.

Every leave he returned to the Island and he always spent his time ashore with the Old Oak for he knew that however long he lived she would still be able to teach him new things. Without fail he also went to see the old lady who gave him his human teaching for he loved the old lady and he used to bring her gifts from the far corners of the world.

Ewan had been promoted to Captain of the Fleet and he was sent on a voyage of discovery in the South Seas and he was away for many years. When he returned to the Island and came to the forest near the grove, he found it was being cut down. A rich landowner had bought the forest and had sent in woodsmen to fell all the trees.

When Ewan saw the trees they were trembling for they knew they were to die. The axemen had cut glades through the forest so that the felled trees could be removed and burned. Already half the forest had gone and he saw men taking away felled trees.

Ewan went to the owner of the forest and pleaded with him to spare the grove at least. But the owner was hard hearted and refused to listen. Though Ewan offered him a high price for the forest, the owner was adamant for he hated sentiment and was angered by Ewan's pleading.

The trees continued to be cut down and Ewan felt helpless to do anything to stop the felling. He slept with his head on the Old Oak and he could feel her trembling and in his dreams he saw that she was terrified, not for herself for she was brave, but for the little trees.

He felt the sadness of the trees all round him and he thought of the Great Tree that had done so much for him, and that his success and happiness in life had come from her wisdom and kindness to him. And now when they called to him for help he was doing nothing for them. He felt bitter despair and helplessness for the very next day the woodsmen would enter the grove of the Old Oak and surely she would be the first to be felled.

He wept when he thought of the death of his teacher, this old oak which he had thought of as his own mother when he had no human mother.

Suddenly an idea came to him. The only path to the grove led past the house of the old lady at the foot of the waterfall. He rose immediately and ran through the steep gorge and reached the house of the old lady.

He told her how the trees of the grove would be cut and how he would like to stop the felling. He offered her a large sum of money for the right of way of the path and the ground leading to the gorge.

The old lady thought of Ewan as her son and she also hated to see the trees cut down so she gladly sold him the right of way for he had also offered far more than she could have got from other men and she was poor and needed help. He thanked her and hurried away for he had much to do before morning when the woodsmen would return.

The woodsmen made their way up the gorge grumbling about the difficulty of removing the trees from the top of the gorge. They had not gone far when they found a barrier in their way, and behind the barrier were sailors from Ewan's ship.

The woodsmen were told that no one would be allowed to pass the barrier so they called for the owner of the forest to come.

The owner was angry with Ewan but he realised that there was no way to get at his trees except through the gorge so he accepted the price Ewan had previously offered.

Ewan having taken possession of the land, restocked the forest and he built a small cottage in the grove so that he and his family, for he had now married, would be sheltered by the leaves of the great Oak and so that they would be able to learn the lessons of the trees.

When he became old and no longer went to sea, he liked nothing more than to dream away the hours beneath the Great Oak and be carried on the dreams of her thoughts, for she taught him all his life long and she thought of him always as her son.

THE QUEEN OF THE WIND

A boy and girl used to go to the end of Bradda Head to watch the sea hurling itself at the cliffs. During storms, Lorna could see figures like huge galleons with heads of astonishing magnificence staring out of the spray and clouds. Only Lorna was able to see the faces - to her the storm came like the navies of Empires.

One stormy day the two children were standing at the foot of the cliffs looking out to sea. Neither of them had seen so fierce a storm and fear gripped them and they fled, seeking shelter under the overhanging walls of the cliffs. Lorna saw the figures as they came towards her and she thought they were searching for something.

And now one of the faces looked directly at her and came swiftly towards her. She turned and ran into a cave, but Patrick did not hear her call of warning nor was he able to see the terrifying face. When Lorna looked back she saw Patrick being carried away by the Storm Lords and she ran out and called his name but her small voice was drowned in the tumult.

No one believed Lorna when she said that Patrick had been carried away by the ships of the Storm and that he was still alive.

Every day she asked her Father, a simple fisherman, to take her to find Patrick, but he would not go for he was afraid of the Storm Lords. Nonetheless he took her with him when he went fishing in his small boat. During every storm she looked into the spray and mist to see if she could see the face of the Storm Lord that had stolen Patrick away from her.

As the days passed and Lorna heard no word of Patrick, she pined for him and became ill and her body became thin and frail. Her Father feared that if he did not take her in search of Patrick, he would surely lose her. So he let her have her way though he feared for both their lives. As soon as she knew that her Father would take her to the land of the Wind, she brightened up and she quickly regained her strength.

Her Father bought provisions for their long voyage and he mended his boat and they set sail. They travelled the oceans of the world and at last they reached a place that was always in storm. When they approached the storm clouds, the boat was thrown about like a leaf and her Father refused to go nearer and turned the bows of the boat away from the storm for fear they would capsize. Lorna urged her Father to sail into the teeth of the storm but he told her it would be the end for both of them.

For many days they circled the storm and always Lorna saw the faces of the Storm Lords. In each face was anger and hatred and in not one of them was pity or compassion.

They reached a gap in the storm clouds. It was like a glade of a forest where the trees have been felled and the wind was rushing into this gap. The boat turned towards the gap and suddenly they were taken by the wind and it was as if they were being driven into the centre of the storm. Around them now were high banks of cloud that reached beyond sight and she saw more clearly than ever the galleons of the Wind and their frightening faces. The boat was now going almost with the speed of the wind and no action of her Father could change its course. He lost hope and turned to Lorna and embraced her and said it was their last moment on Earth.

The darkness and noise made Lorna think they had reached the end of the Earth. The boat was going faster and faster and it shuddered and twisted and lurched and her Father was thrown down and his head struck the mast and he lay senseless. Lorna went to him quickly and held him in her arms but no life was in him. Bitter sorrow came to Lorna for it was her stubbornness that had made him come to the Land of the Wind.

After many hours the Storm abated and the boat steadied and the wind lessened and it became bright for the sun shone through the clouds. Soon she saw blue sky and the sea under the boat became as the sky. Now the wind fell and the boat touched a sandy beach in a lagoon. She lowered herself to the beach and walked across a strip of sand and climbed a dune from where she could see a green valley. In the distance she heard the sound of a storm but here it was calm. When she walked in the valley she found that its trees were bowed down with fruit of all kinds. After the long sea voyage with the dry shipboard food, she was hungry for fruit and she ate greedily. It was warm and she felt her spirits revive a little. Far away across the valley was a small hut and hope rose in her and she ran towards it. Inside a frail creature stood up and she scarcely recognised Patrick for he was thin and pale like the wind. She kissed him and said she had come to take him home.

After a dazed silence he spoke to her slowly. His voice came to her as a whispering of wind in dry grass.

He looked sad when he spoke. 'Save yourself if you can, for me it is too late for they have turned me into a creature of the wind by their magic and I will die if I am taken away from here.

She feared what he had said for he was a shadow of what he had been and he had a deathly pallor about his face. She felt sorrow and dread. But she was determined to save him and she took his thin hand and led him away from the hut. She said that if they could reach the lagoon they would be safe for they could sail away in the boat.

But he whispered again that no one who stays on the Island of the Wind has ever returned to the world of men.

Again fear came to her when she heard what he said but she would not believe him. Already he was weakening and she had to drag him towards the

71

ship and she had to stop often to regain her breath.

At last they reached the top of the dune but when Lorna looked towards the lagoon, the ship was gone. She dropped to the ground bewildered and downcast. She looked all round her in despair and it was as if she heard the sound of laughter in the howling of the wind in the distance.

It had taken her a long time to bring Patrick to the dune and it was now evening and the sun was setting. They could see nothing all round them except a small cloud on the horizon. It came towards them and Patrick said it was the messenger of the Queen of the Wind. The cloud came nearer and its shape of a funnel could be seen clearly. The whirlwind was gathering speed as it approached and Lorna turned to run but Patrick told her to stay for no one escapes the messenger of the Queen.

The sound of the whirlwind increased and the hissing became so loud that nothing could be heard above it and they could feel the wind clutching at their clothes. Suddenly they were lifted off their feet and they felt themselves soaring into the heavens. Up and up they went and now it was like night, so thick was the spray and the clouds and the sand. Soon they felt cold, and still they went up and up. The spray about them turned to hail and the cold became intense and then the noise of the whirlwind ended and they were put down gently on the floor of a huge building of ice.

Far above them on a platform was a throne and on it sat a figure in black with wild hair. On her head was a crown shining with dark jewels. Greatness was in her look and power so that fear came upon Lorna. They climbed the steps to the throne and the Queen rose and carressed Patrick and when her cold hand touched his head he shivered.

She spoke with the Voices of the Wind. She lisped and the words sounded like the wind in a forest. Sometimes her voice rose in a moaning sound that told Lorna of power and determination that was immeasurable. Patrick told Lorna what the Queen of the Wind said, 'Why have you come to my land? Is it to steal Patrick away who is my only human companion?'

Lorna trembled for she knew that if she said anything to cause anger, she might be killed so cruel were the eyes of the Queen of the Wind. Lorna hesitated and then said, 'I came to see if Patrick was alive. He is ill and will not live unless he is given more food for we people of the land cannot live on fruit alone. It is also too cold for him in this court of ice.'

The Queen said, 'I will not make him come here so often. I want you to look after him and feed him so that he will be strong again. During the day you will always stay in the Valley of the Fruit trees in the warmth, you need come to me only in the night.'

She had a coldness in her voice as if her heart was of ice. Lorna said, 'What has become of my Father?'

The Queen lisped again in her strange voice of the wind and Patrick told Lorna what had been said. 'We did not want him to stay here so we revived him by magic and sent him home. The Wind Lords have been ordered to speed him on his journey.'

Lorna asked the Queen if she and Patrick would ever be allowed to return home.

The Queen said, 'This is Patrick's home. It is a paradise which no one ever wishes to leave. Have we not got trees of all the countries of the world that bear fruit all the year long? Is not the valley in which you and Patrick stay always sunny and warm? In our land is no dust or hunger or thirst or want or disease. You will learn to be happy just as Patrick is happy and you will never want to leave us. So sure of this am I that at the end of a year, I will let you choose whether you want to stay or leave.'

While the Queen spoke, Lorna watched her and she knew that the Queen was not telling the truth. The Queen would never release Patrick and they were prisoners. Lorna could read the Queen's heart and it was like a leaf dried by the merciless wind.

Patrick and Lorna were now tired from the struggles of the day and the Queen sent for the whirlwind to take them away to the Valley of the Fruit trees.

They lived on the Island of the Wind and each day Lorna looked after Patrick but despite the food she gave him and the care she lavished on him; he did not thrive. The coldness of the Queen's court and the sound of the wind and the loneliness had taken his courage away. Each evening when the sun went down, the whirlwind came to bring them to the Queen's court of ice where they were entertained by the sound of the orchestra of the wind. The music was the sound of snow and hail falling through thin strands of air, and the breath of the Wind Lords passing through the organ pipes of icicles. Sometimes the music swelled with the songs of the Bugganes, the children of the Wind, with their high pitched voices.

After Lorna had been going to the concerts for some time the Queen spoke to her in a voice that had in it a trace of triumph. 'No one who has listened to the music of the Wind will ever be able to return to the world of men. Now you are like Patrick and will become one of the creatures of the wind, which are as thoughts of mine. You are one of us and you will want only to stay with us here in the Island of the Wind and live amongst us who are your own people.'

But Lorna had suspected and feared the music of the Wind and when she had been taken to the concerts she had put locks of hair in her ears. Instead of listening to the music, she pretended to listen, and she watched Patrick who seemed to be drugged and each time he heard the music he became even more frail and more like the wind. She knew with dread that it would not be long before he was one of the creatures of the wind, and would be as frail as the eddying gusts of air.

Every night they were brought to listen to the music and they were told sad stories by the Queen of the Wind - stories that chilled their souls and long before dawn they became cold and lifeless.

The Queen kissed Patrick and smiled her cold smile for she knew that his lips were nearly as cold as hers and he would soon be one of her children of the Wind.

Now the messenger of the whirlwind lifted up their lifeless bodies and took them to the Valley of the Fruit Trees, and there the Sun in his compassion rose early and warmed them and brought them back to life. Lorna thought of themselves as puppets of the Queen that were frozen and brought back to life again by the Sun in the morning.

Day followed day and now Lorna was almost as thin as Patrick and she despaired for she saw no hope for them. One day they were carried up to the Courts of Ice but the Queen of the Wind was not there on her high throne and in her place was the Lord of the West Wind. Lorna recognised the face of the Storm Lord who had captured Patrick. His voice was like the wildest storms though it was not so shrill and powerful as the voice of the Queen of the Wind.

He had seen Lorna often and he had learned to like her and admire her and he said, 'You are a brave girl to come to the Land of the Wind to rescue Patrick. You are brave but foolish. Because you are so brave, it may be that you would like to come with me on my journeys round the world. I will show you all the countries of the East and the West, we will go to the Antarctic where no men live and we will see China and all the Islands of the Pacific.'

He had majesty and irresistable power in his speech and bearing. She feared him but she was overwhelmed with admiration for she recognised in him one of the Great Lords of the Earth. Though she feared for her life, she could not prevent herself saying she would be honoured to go with him. But she said she could only go if Patrick also went. When she mentioned Patrick, she saw a change in the face of the Lord of the West Wind for even he feared the wrath of the Queen of the Wind.

Time passed and now the climate changed for the Islands of the Wind moved towards the North and the winds changed and the weather, except in the Valley of the Fruit trees, became colder. The Lord of the West Wind showed Lorna how the Island went from one end of the Earth to the other. He took her into the deep mines of the Island where the winds were made and forced by huge bellows into gigantic windbags that were stored until they were needed. The winds in the underground passages were so strong that the Lord of the West Wind had to hold Lorna to prevent her from being broken against the ice walls.

He spoke of the children of the Wind, the Bugganes. 'Some of them are princelings whose power is almost as great as that of the South Wind. And some of the bugganes are no more than small children. When the Queen is angry she sends me, the Lord of the West Wind, to chastise her enemies; but if the transgression is small, she sends only the bugganes who can destroy houses and remove their roofs. The smallest bugganes are very small so they can do only mischievous pranks such as turning umbrellas outside in or blowing old folks' hats into the sea.'

Time after time the Lord of the West Wind asked Lorna to accompany him, and again and again she refused unless Patrick went with them. In his mind the Lord of the West Wind wrestled with his desire to take Lorna with him and his fear of the Queen of the Wind.

One day the Queen of the Wind left Court to visit her dominions and with her went the armies of the Wind and most of the Bugganes, all except the Lord of the West Wind and his army, which was ordered to stay and guard the Island of the Wind.

No sooner had the Queen left than the Lord of the West Wind saw his opportunity to take Lorna and Patrick with him. He gathered his army and sent the messenger of the Whirlwind to bring Lorna and Patrick to him and he set out in his galleon. True to his word, he showed Lorna all the countries of the world. They saw the Pacific, and the Antarctic and China. In time Lorna became tired of the long journey and she was homesick so she asked the Lord of the West Wind to bring them to see the Isle of Man for the last time, for she knew that she would never again see it once she returned to the Island of the Wind. Once more the Lord of the West Wind changed the course of the storm clouds and the galleon was lifted up and they went swiftly to the North.

As they approached the Isle of Man, they became aware of a storm on the horizon. At first the Lord of the West Wind looked at it with disdain but soon his look of power changed, and fear came to him so threatening was the storm and so dark the sky. They sped in terror towards the Island but the storm followed and overtook them. Panic gripped the host of the West Wind and the Bugganes were scattered and the Lord of the West Wind lost his look of power and greatness for he knew now that his pursuer was the Queen of the Wind who had come in her wrath because of Patrick.

The galleon of the West Wind was broken on the cliffs and the Lord of the West Wind tried to carry Lorna with him but she was torn from his grasp and he fled. Lorna found herself on the sea shore with Patrick and they struggled towards the cliffs and reached a cave where they sought shelter, and they waited for the Queen of the Wind to come for them. But she was so angry with the West Wind that she had no eyes for Patrick hiding in the cave and she wished only to punish the Lord of the West Wind for disobeying her commands.

The storm increased in the Island and hardly a roof of a single house was not blown away. The Queen raved about the Island flashing her torch of the lightning in search of the West Wind. At last she caught him and chastised him and her anger abated and she left the Island.

Lorna and Patrick reached their homes and Lorna was greeted by her Father as if she was returned from the dead. Her Father could not contain his joy for he had been sad and lonely since he lost Lorna and now his life was transformed and happiness filled his days. Patrick also founds happiness for an old wise woman who understood magic spells was able to break his enchantment by the music of the Wind and he became strong again.

When they grew up, Patrick and Lorna married but the Queen of the Wind never stopped looking for Patrick, and always when a storm came to the Island, Patrick and Lorna hid until the storm left for fear the eyes of the Queen of the Wind should fall on them again.

THE FORTUNATE ISLES

An old Sea Captain lived in a small cottage near the harbour at Peel. His name was Adam but no one called him that for as long as men could remember he had been the Captain. All the people of the town avoided him for he was considered strange and eccentric and some people even supposed him to be mad.

Though the adults of the town did not speak to him, the children loved to go to his cottage and listen to the stories he told them. One of the boys was named Brennan and at first he went to the Captain's cottage only to hear the stories but later he felt pity for the old man and began to help with the chores and he cooked the old man's food and fetched his shopping.

They became friends and each day long after the other children had left to go to their homes, Brennan and the Captain continued to talk. A few years passed and one day the Captain told Brennan who was now a young man that he intended to sell his cottage and buy an ocean going boat. He said he hoped they would sail together on a long voyage. It had always been one of Brennan's ambitions to learn to navigate and to sail a ship so he was delighted, but he wondered if the Captain was being foolish selling his cottage and sailing away when he was already an old man.

The Captain saw the expression of concern and he smiled and gave his reason for what he wanted to do in a story of his life:

'I had been sailing for many years and I had become the Master of a ship bound for the Pacific. We rounded the Horn and as always I felt relief for no Captain goes round the Horn without some misgivings. Even as I gave thanks for the safety of my ship and my crew, it came to me with foreboding that this was not to be a happy voyage. I became perplexed and worried and this troubled me for never before had I felt fear except when face to face with danger.

'We sailed for months and charted the Islands that we reached, and since no danger threatened and all was well my fears lessened.

'But one night a storm suddenly arose and our ship was driven onto a submerged reef and she was split open and started to break up. I saw the last of the men safely off the ship and I lowered myself into a ship's boat.

'The storm increased and we lost contact with the other boats. At last. the storm lessened and we rigged a sail and steered towards Australia far away to the South West. At first we made good progress for the wind was favourable but a dead calm set in and the sea became motionless like a stagnant pool. The fresh water we had collected during the storm began to run out and we caught no more fish, and we prayed for rain and wind. After a week men started to die and a day came when only two of us were left on the boat. I knew that we could not survive another night, and I felt pity for the young man who was with me

77

for he was barely at the threshold of manhood,

'I lay down and slept for a few hours and when I woke, I sensed some movement of the boat; and even in my dazed state, I felt the wonder of it for no wind was in the sail and not a single ripple was on the surface of the sea. I thought the movement was a hallucination for I had had many strange reveries and I had seen phantasms during my extreme thirst.

'The boat nonetheless continued to move steadily hour after hour and the time was approaching morning. I knew that the dawn could not be far off and I remember my surprise for I had thought that I should surely not see another dawn. I felt relief and rapture and an intense desire to reach the place to which the boat was bound for I knew without any doubt that it was not going aimlessly. I was stronger now and my thirst had lessened and I felt no more pain. In my joy at the hope of reaching a place of wonder and delight I thought of my young companion but when I shook him by the shoulder he did not stir and I knew he was dead. I lay down once more saddened.

'Much later the increasing brightness caused me to stand up and I saw far away a light shining on the horizon. I discerned the outlines of Islands. I searched for them on the chart but could not find them. When I looked at the compass, the needle would not settle. I stared at the instrument in amazement for there was no metal on the boat. I looked at the islands again and I knew that no such Islands were on the charts.

'I sensed the wonder of it for it was supernatural and I realised that I was in a place that was no where. I had passed beyond the charts of men and I felt hope and awe. After my many years of responsibility and worry and concern, I was free for I had reached a land where all I knew was of no avail and I was beyond the jurisdiction of men. I abandoned myself with thanksgiving and relief.

'The boat had advanced steadily in the direction of the light. As it neared the Islands the brilliance of the light astonished me for it was not of the same quality as man-made light; and my eyes became strained looking at it, 'Soon the boat grated on sharp sand and, I must have been overcome for I can remember little of that moment. Just as I was falling unconscious I was vaguely aware of beautiful beings helping me from the boat and they took me to a house that seemed to be transparent and I was clothed in silken clothing.

'After the hardships and the fears of the voyage and the shipwreck, I was utterly at peace as if I had reached a place where danger was no more. I slept for very long and when I woke I felt refreshed and happy as I had never felt before, and I had a joyful feeling of health and vitality. A woman who was to be my guide told me that I had reached the Fortunate Isles which are the heaven of the brave of the sea, and that I had come home.

'Her talk made me suppose that I was dead and I felt no sorrow. The beauty of the people confirmed my thought for they were too perfect to have been of the Earth. It was a land of perpetual youth without sickness, or death, or age.

'I asked the beautiful guide who she was and where the people had come from. Etain, for that was her name, smiled at me and told me this story: "Long ago in the time when the Gods were young and when few people were on the Earth, one of the Gods said that the reason for the wickedness of men was that they had no beautiful things to occupy their thoughts. He told the other Gods that if they were to build a garden of Paradise, men would see its beauty and try to emulate it in their own lives.

"So the Gods built a paradise. The flowers of that garden were not like earthly flowers for they had the colours of the rainbow, and they existed in a mysterious place that was on the borderlands of the senses. The flowers were so beautiful that men would become dazed in looking at them.

"When the King of the Gods saw the men enamoured of the flowers of the Garden of Paradise he was pleased but he thought that something was still lacking, and he decided that a woman should be in the garden worthy of the beauty of the flowers. He commanded that she was to be the most beautiful woman who ever was or ever will be and she was to be made by the Gods of flowers.

"Marvellous workmen of heaven strove for many years of heavenly time to design the face of Blodeuwedd. At last they were satisfied with their creation and they showed her to the Gods. The face of Blodeuwedd was not the face of mortal beauty but of all beauty. Everyone who saw Blodeuwedd read in her features the face of his own lover transfigured and made more perfect. An aura like the rainbow was about Blodeuwedd and no one could say he had truly seen her for she shimmered like the mirage. The scent of the Garden of Paradise and the spell cast by Blodeuwedd made every man who entered the garden and behold her face fall down and become senseless. Some men tried to look at her in a mirror but it was of no avail; all who discerned her face became caught in subtle chains of power and they became the helpless lovers of Blodeuwedd. Soon many men were in the garden of the Gods and they had only strength enough to eat the ambrosial fruit and rest and they waited craving a glimpse of the face of Blodeuwedd.

"In that country were two brothers and a sister whose father was the King. The Princes were twins and no one except their sister could tell them apart.

'"The elder brother Edward heard of the beauty of Blodeuwedd and he resolved that he would try to rescue the suitors from the Garden of Paradise and perhaps win Blodeuwedd for himself.

"When Edward entered the Garden, Blodeuwedd saw him and she was

79

struck by his appearance for he was more handsome than all the men she had ever met. She feared that if he saw her face he would become like all the other lost lovers so she hid herself from him and watched from a distance. Each day she looked at him from a high window of the palace which was set in the middle of the garden of Paradise, She looked at him in rapture hour after hour. For many days she watched Edward without herself being seen but one day while she was watching, a bird flew up out of a tree above her head and she looked up startled. At that same instant Edward also looked up and he saw Blodeuwedd and he fell down senseless. Blodeuwedd was sad and bitterly regretted her tragic beauty.

"When Edward did not return to the palace of the King, Edmond the brother knew that Blodeuwedd must have bewitched Edward in the Garden of Paradise and he decided to go to the rescue.

"But his sister sought to dissuade him for she could not believe that the blind prince Edmond would succeed where his brother had failed. Edmond though he was blind had in him the blood of heroes so he told his sister that it did not matter if he, a blind man were to be lost, and this was a chance for him to make something of his life by helping his brother.

"Edmond was led into the garden by a page and as they entered the gates Blodeuwedd who was still heart broken by the loss of Edward saw Edmond in the distance. She thought he was Edward recovered from the spell and she went to him quickly, and though Edmond could not see her, he sensed the beauty of her soul and he was overwhelmed with the sweetness of her speech and her kindness. It was not long before they were married and from that day onward, Blodeuwedd aged a little each day, whereas before that time she had lived in Paradise for many years and men thought she had the secret of eternal youth.

"Blodeuwedd was made of flowers and like the flowers her seed time had come and she wilted. Day followed day and each day some of her beauty left her. The colour of her face dimmed and the glimmer of the deep pools of her eyes dulled. Soon she was no longer beautiful, and some of the suitors who had been made helpless by her charms began to stir and come out of the dreams into which they had been plunged, and the spells gradually wore off and one by one they left the garden. Each time Blodeuwedd became uglier more of the suitors left and a time came when no one was with her except the blind prince Edmond. They were happy together for Edmond could not see the ugliness of Blodeuwedd and he saw only the inner beauty; for all the beauty of Blodeuwedd was never lost for it went inward and the Prince knew that he had married the most beautiful woman who ever was.

"Long afterwards the garden seemed to recede and the scent of the flowers was only a memory; for the garden, which was on several islands left the mainland and soon it could no longer be seen on the horizon and men of the land were never to see it again. The islands went far away into the deep ocean of the Pacific and strange to say Blodeuwedd and Edmond changed for she regained her beauty and Edmond was able to see.

"The garden of the Gods became the Fortunate Isles and whenever brave men are lost at sea the daughters of Blodeuwedd rescue them. When those brave sailors reach the Fortunate Isles their faces are made luminous like the face of Edmond and they are comforted by the daughters of Blodeuwedd."

The Captain paused for a moment and then continued.

'When Etain had finished her story and even long before she had finished it, I knew that I was as enamoured of her as Edmond was of Blodeuwedd. And I was astonished when she said that she loved me also."

'Etain and I were happy in those gardens of the Fortunate Isles and I hoped that I would spend all eternity with her, for there was no death or sickness or sorrow in the Fortunate Isles.

'But one day I was told that I had to return to the world of men for they had made a mistake and my time for leaving the world had not yet come. I was sad for the thought of going back to the darkness and ignorance of men from the light and beauty of the Fortunate Isles was terrible to me. Etain held me and comforted me and said that it would not be long - not long compared to the eternity we should spend together afterwards. And then she told me something that seemed at the time to me to be very unusual and it was that I should forget all I had seen in the Fortunate Isles and that I should go back and be as cheerful as I could be and marry and live happily on the Earth.

'And to tell the truth, for many years I forgot all I had seen on the Islands but never the face of Etain. The form of her face was branded on my mind and that is why I have never married.'

The Captain paused again and then he said, 'During the past few weeks I have felt the same passionate desire for the Fortunate Isles as I felt in the boat as I neared them after the shipwreck. And now in my dreams I see more and more clearly the face of Etain who calls for me. My time has come to leave and I must hasten away to the Fortunate Isles. Are you coming with me or must I go alone?'

Brennan had no thought of not going, and he could think of nothing he would rather do, and he had a strong affection for the old man that made it a duty for him to go.

They bought a boat and rigged her and set sail to the South. After many months they rounded the Horn and entered the Pacific. The Captain had aged rapidly and now each day showed a change, and Brennan wondered if the old man would live long enough to reach the Fortunate Isles. The Captain became so weak that Brennan did all the work of the ship while the Captain rested.

One day as Brennan was doing the chores on deck, he looked at his friend in pity. Tears were welling from the old eyes and yet he was asleep. Profound sorrow stirred in Brennan and when the Captain awoke, Brennan said, 'How sorry I feel for you, what a tragedy was your visit to the Fortunate Isles for it ruined your life on the Earth, You have never married and had children and none of the things men strive for has meant anything for you so you have lived a meaningless life.'

The old Captain smiled at Brennan and said, 'You are wrong. You must not think that I have been unhappy. You have seen the tears well from my eyes and soak my pillow and often this happens to me and when I wake, I feel no sorrow and I am happy. Those tears come from another world to which I go in sleep and they are tears of joy, not of sadness. It is true that my visit to the Fortunate Isles deprived me of the desire for success in the world, and for that reason I must tell you not to look at the beings who live there. But my life has not been sad, for I knew that I was from another world which is far more wonderful and perfect than the world of men. So I have been untroubled by men's unkindness to me. Sometimes I have seen visions of the Fortunate Isles like a shaft of sunlight that surprises one in the darkness of winter. I cannot be unhappy for I am going home, and far away I possess a wife who is immortal and soon I will be with her and we shall be happy for ever.'

Now the Captain saw in his dreams the people more clearly and he knew that he was nearing the Fortunate Isles. Another day passed and the Captain had become so old and feeble that he was on the point of death. He spoke to Brennan taking him by the hand, 'You are the last and best friend I have ever had. And now I must leave you. The boat is yours and you have earned it not only because of your steadfastness but for your mastery of navigation and seamanship. Be brave and one day we will meet again in the Fortunate Isles.'

In the darkness Brennan lowered the ship's boat into the sea and placed the Captain gently into it and said farewell.

The little boat went towards the distant light and Brennan marvelled for there was no wind and the sea was calm. He looked for a long time and just as the boat was going out of sight, he saw a figure of a young man standing in the boat and waving to him. Now far away he could hear the sound of music that lingered in his mind all his life. He felt overwhelmed by the scent of paradisaic flowers. Slowly he sailed away in the ship and soon he could no longer hear the music of the Fortunate Isles.

Tir-Nan-Og, Land of the Ever Young.
A short Sequel to Children of Darkland.

Ian, Arawa and Findavir became heroes of the Battles of the Darkland but they were so injured that they no longer wished to remain on Earth. Such people could go to the Celtic World of Tir-Nan-Og which was the land of the ever young. They left Danaia accompanied by many Danaians on the short distance to the Emerald Sea, where a small boat was waiting in readiness with a crew of oarsmen. The Danaians were full of joy because to them leaving the world and going to other worlds was the culmination of the happy life and its greatest reward.

The boat was cast off and sped out of sight of the Danaians on the shore. It went on and on until they saw a mysterious light far ahead of them. It approached rapidly and soon they were able to make out the shape of a ship, but such a ship as they had never before seen.

They went alongside and they were beckoned to come aboard. On the ship was a woman of the fairest form, who gave them each three gifts. The first was a golden goblet, which could change water to wine: the wine of forgetfulness of self, so that no sorrow would ever again visit them. The second gift was a golden apple, which conferred eternal life; no sooner had they taken one bite than they were transformed and all their sicknesses and pain left them. The third gift was a golden bough, which was a talisman, a passport, conferring on them the right of those who were still alive to enter Tir-Nan-Og. The golden apples not only conferred immortality but they were the sustenance for the journey for however much was eaten it would not diminish in size.

In joy they ate the apples and sped over the sea. They reached an Island through mist, which never lifted to disclose the Island's form. The scent was so ravishing that they thought that they had already reached Tir-Nan-Og and they swooned and went into a profound sleep. This was the Celtic Island of the Lotus eaters, and they were drawn into regions of dreams and endless slumber, but the ship took them safely past and soon they were beyond the influence of the Island.

When they woke they were no longer in the Darkland but were sailing on a boundless sea, the Western Ocean of Manannan. Mariners of their magic ship had hoisted sails and it was moving so swiftly that they feared it would be destroyed.

They came through mist to a land fairer than any they had ever seen or imagined. They stopped at a shore where youths and maidens of surpassing grace welcomed them with fruit and drink. All about them was music that seemed to come from the very sand and waves of the sea.

Suddenly they were clothed in green and found themselves walking in groves of trees whose fruit never failed for even when one was picked it would be replaced by the next morning.They walked so lightly in the heavenly air that the grass and flowers were not pressed beneath their feet.

They were bathed in a spring, which was the Fountain of Perpetual youth. After their bath and when they were cleansed of all earthly dross and defilement, they were clothed in shining robes by the Ever Young who escorted them to the court of the Queen of Tir-Nan-Og,

From that day on they were happy all their days and they were together in the perpetual springtime of Tir-Nan-Og.

****